THE GLENCOE LITERATURE LIBRARY

The Slave Dancer

and Related Readings

Glencoe
McGraw-Hill

New York, New York   Columbus, Ohio   Woodland Hills, California   Peoria, Illinois

Acknowledgments

Grateful acknowledgment is given authors, publishers, photographers, museums, and agents for permission to reprint the following copyrighted material. Every effort has been made to determine copyright owners. In case of any omissions, the Publisher will be pleased to make suitable acknowledgments in future editions.

SLAVE DANCER by Paula Fox. This edition is reprinted by arrangement with Simon & Schuster Books for Young Readers, Simon & Schuster Children's Publishing Division. Copyright © 1973 by Paula Fox. Copyright © renewed 1999, by Paula Fox. All rights reserved.

Text excerpts "Red Caps in the Mist," "War Drums," and "In Camp with the Enemy" from ESCAPE FROM THE SLAVE TRADERS by Dave and Neta Jackson. Copyright © 1992, Bethany House Publishers. Reprinted by permission.

"The Fiery Abolitionists" reprinted with the permission of Atheneum Books for Young Readers, an imprint of Simon & Schuster Children's Publishing Division from BREAKING THE CHAINS by William Loren Katz. Copyright © 1990 Ethrac Publications, Inc.

"Afro-American Fragment" and "American Heartbreak" from COLLECTED POEMS by Langston Hughes. Copyright © 1994 by the Estate of Langston Hughes. Reprinted by permission of Alfred A. Knopf, Inc.

Leta Gray (Interviewer) May 17, 1937 for the American Guide, Topeka, Kansas. Person interviewed in Ottawa, Kansas.

From RETURN WITH HONOR by Scott O'Grady. Copyright © 1995 by Scott O'Grady. Used by permission of Doubleday, a division of Random House, Inc.

Cover Art: Christie's Images/Bridgeman Art Library

Glencoe/McGraw-Hill

A Division of The **McGraw·Hill** Companies

Send all inquiries to:
Glencoe/McGraw-Hill
8787 Orion Place
Columbus, Ohio 43240

ISBN 0-02-818004-6
Printed in the United States of America
3 4 5 6 7 8 9 026 04 03 02 01

Contents

The Slave Dancer

Related Readings

Continued

Contents *Continued*

The Slave Dancer

Paula Fox

History

Ship	*The Moonlight*
Officers	Captain Cawthorne—the Master
	Nicholas Spark—the Mate
Crew	Jessie Bollier
	John Cooley
	Adolph Curry
	Louis Gardere
	Ned Grime
	Isaac Porter
	Clay Purvis
	Claudius Sharkey
	Seth Smith
	Benjamin Stout
	Sam Wick
Cargo	98 slaves whose true names were remembered only by their families, except for the young boy, Ras

Shipwrecked in the Gulf of Mexico, June 3, 1840

Survivors	2

The Errand

IN A HINGED WOODEN BOX upon the top of which was carved a winged fish, my mother kept the tools of her trade. Sometimes I touched a sewing needle with my finger and reflected how such a small object, so nearly weightless, could keep our little family from the poorhouse and provide us with enough food to sustain life—although there were times when we were barely sustained.

Our one room was on the first floor of a brick and timber house which must have seen better times. Even on sunny days I could press my hand against the wall and force the moisture which coated it to run to the floor in streams. The damp sometimes set my sister, Betty, to coughing which filled the room with barking noises like those made by quarreling animals. Then my mother would mention how fortunate we were to live in New Orleans where we did not suffer the cruel extremes of temperature that prevailed in the north. And when it rained for days on end, leaving behind when it ceased a green mold which clung to my boots, the walls and even the candlesticks, my mother thanked God that we were spared the terrible blizzards she remembered from her childhood in Massachusetts. As for the fog, she observed how it softened the clamor from the streets and alleyways and kept the drunken riverboat men away from our section of the *Vieux Carré*.

I disliked the fog. It made me a prisoner. I imagined, sitting there on a bench in the shadows of the little room, that the smoky yellow stuff which billowed against our two windows was a kind of sweat thrown off by the Mississippi River as it coiled and twisted toward the sea.

Except for the wooden sewing box, a sea chest which had belonged to my mother's father, and her work table, we owned scarcely anything. One cupboard held the few scraps of our linen, the cooking pots and implements, candle ends and a bottle of burning liquid which my mother rubbed on Betty's chest when she was feverish. There were two chamber pots on the floor, hidden by day in the shadow of the cupboard but clearly visible by candlelight, the white porcelain one chipped and discolored, the other decorated with a painting of an ugly orange flower which my mother said was a lily.

There was one pretty object in the room, a basket of colored spools of thread which sat on the sill of the window facing Pirate's Alley. By candlelight, the warmth of the colors made me think the thread would throw off a perfume like a garden of flowers.

But these spools were not used for our clothes. They were for the silks and muslins and laces which my mother made into gowns for the rich ladies of New Orleans to wear to their balls and receptions, their weddings and the baptism of their infants, and sometimes to their funerals.

One early evening toward the end of January, I walked slowly home inventing a story that might distract my mother from asking me why I was late and where I had been. I was relieved to find her so pre-occupied there was no need to tell her anything. Even if I had blurted out the truth—that I had spent an hour wandering about the slave market at the corner of St. Louis and Chartres Streets, a place as strictly forbidden to me as Congo Square, where slaves were allowed to hold their festivities, I doubt she would have heard me. The whole room was covered with a great swath of apricot colored brocade sup-ported by chairs to keep it from touching the floor. Betty crouched in a corner, staring at the cloth as though in a daze, while my mother, her back against the wall, gripped an edge of the brocade in her two hands and shook her head from side to side, muttering to herself in words I could not make out.

I had seen damask and gauze and velvet and silk across my mother's knees or falling in cascades from her table, but never such a lavish piece as this, of such a radiant hue. Designs were embroidered upon it showing lords and ladies bowing, and prancing horses no larger than thimbles, their rear hooves buried in flowers, haloes of birds and butterflies circling their caparisoned heads.

Without looking up, my mother said, "We need more candles," in such a fretful and desperate voice, I knew she was pressed for time and had before her a piece of work that would keep her up many nights.

I held out a few coins. I had earned them that afternoon playing my fife for the steamboat crews who came to gorge themselves on the fruit that was sold in the great market near the levee.

She glanced at my hand. "Not enough," she said. "Go and bor-row some from Aunt Agatha. I must start work on this nightmare right away."

"It's beautiful!" cried Betty.

"This nightmare . . ." repeated my mother wearily.

I hesitated. I hated to go to Aunt Agatha's neat house on St. Ann Street. No matter how often I went, my aunt would always direct my course like a pilot boat as soon as I opened the door. "Don't walk there!" she would cry. "Take your huge feet off that carpet! Watch the chair—it'll fall! Can't you walk like a gentleman instead of some lout from the bayou?"

To Betty and my mother, I called her a disagreeable and mean old maid. My mother replied that I was a surly boy and would grow up to become an uncharitable man. She was, after all, my mother said, my father's only living relative, and her grief at his death had entirely changed her nature. "We're his relatives," I'd muttered. That was different, she'd said. Still, I had no other memory of Aunt Agatha except as a woman who especially disliked me.

I had been four, and Betty a month from being born, when my father drowned in the Mississippi River. He had been working on a snagboat, helping to clear away the tree stumps and other hidden de- bris that had made the river so perilous for the passage of steamboats. The snagboat had been caught by a current, my father lost his foot- ing, fell and sank before anyone could help him.

In dreams, sometimes even when I was fully awake, a voice inside my head would cry, "Oh, swim!" as though by such an appeal I could make the river return my father to us. Once my mother had heard this involuntary cry escape my lips. "He was brave," she had said. But I was not comforted. "He is dead," I had said.

My mother had reminded me then that there were souls whose fates were so terrible in comparison to ours, that we should consider ourselves among the fortunate of the earth. I knew she was thinking of the slaves who were sold daily so close to where we lived.

"Jessie! Will you go now, this instant?"

"I've a cramp in my leg," Betty complained.

"Well then, stand up, girl," said my mother crossly.

I went out onto the street wondering what she would have said if she'd known that this very day I'd seen six Africans offered up for sale as cane hands. They had been dressed as if they had been going to a ball, even to the white gloves they were all wearing. "These niggers are matchless!" the auctioneer had cried, at which instant I was picked up bodily by a man as hairy as a dray horse, thrown to the pavement and told to keep away from the slave market until I had something better in mind than nasty peeking.

I knew the way so well, my feet took me to Aunt Agatha's without help from my brain. She received me in her usual fashion, then gave me three candles.

"Why doesn't your mother use her oil lamps?" she asked accusingly.

"They smoke," I answered.

"They wouldn't if someone knew how to trim them properly."

"They don't give enough light," I said.

"People shouldn't work at night anyhow," she said, then, catching sight of the fife which I always carried, she exclaimed, "What an undignified way to earn your keep! Playing that silly pipe! It's time you were apprenticed and learned a trade. I doubt you'd benefit from schooling."

"My mother has taught me reading and numbers," I answered as sharply as I dared.

"But who is to teach you how to think?" she snapped back.

I could think of no answer to that so I made for the door, remembering to sidestep a small carpet she prized. "Goodnight, Auntie," I said, as though I were about to burst into laughter. I heard her snort as I closed the door.

The night sky was clear. The air was faintly scented with the aroma of flowers which grew in such profusion inside the walled gardens that belonged to the rich families in our neighborhood. Often I had climbed those walls and peered through the black iron grille work into the great rooms of their houses or looked down into the gardens where, among the beds of flowers, a stone hut had been piled up to shelter the house slaves. Once I had seen a lady glide across a floor in a gown I was sure my mother had made, and on another evening I had been startled when, thinking myself unobserved, I had grown aware of a silent watcher, a black woman who stood leaning against the doorless entrance of such a hut. She had been utterly still; her arms hanging straight by her sides, her eyes fixed upon me as I half straddled the wall.

I had been afraid she would suddenly decide to give the alarm, and I was angry she had seen me at all. "Star!" someone had called, and at that, the black woman had placed her hands on her hips and, without a glance in my direction, moved toward the house.

I had never heard anyone called such a name before. When I told my mother about it, omitting the circumstances in which I'd heard it, she said, "Might as well call someone 'shoe'. It's not a human name."

For a while, I didn't climb garden walls. But the memory of the woman standing there in the evening shadows stayed with me. I wondered why her master had called her Star, and what she had thought about her name and if she thought about it at all, and I often recalled how she'd walked so slowly and silently to the big house, her skirt hiding the movement of her feet so that she seemed to float across the ground.

I felt restless, and reluctant to return to the room full of brocade, so I took the longest way home, using alleys that kept me off the main streets where sailors and gentlemen and chandlers and cotton merchants and farmers went to make themselves drunk in taverns, and where women gotten up like parrots kept them company.

My mother, repeating the Sunday warnings of the parson about the sinfulness of our quarter, had asked me to promise her I would never enter a tavern or mingle with the nightly throngs on Bourbon and Royal Streets. By keeping to these narrow byways, I avoided breaking the promise but still had the diversion of hearing from over the rooftops the rumble and rise and fall of men's voices, the bird shrieks of women, laughter and the shouts of quarrels and the abrupt iron-like strokes of horses' hooves on cobblestones, as the horsemen set off toward unknown destinations.

Someday, I might become a rich chandler in a fine suit, with a thousand candles to hand if I needed them instead of three grudgingly given stubs. I imagined the splendid house I would live in, my gardens, my carriage and horses. I was so intoxicated by my vision that I rose up on my toes as though to meet the fate I had invented. What I encountered was foul smelling canvas, a sky full of it, covering me entirely, forcing me to the ground.

I heard men's voices. Hands gripped me through the canvas. I was tossed, then trussed, then lifted up and carried like a pig to market.

"Take up that pipe, Claudius," a voice growled near my bound head. "He's worth nothing without his pipe!"

"I don't see it," said another voice in a complaining gurgle.

I was dropped on the ground, and the canvas loosened around my face. I tried to shout but the musty cloth filled my mouth and I could get no air into my lungs. My limbs were twisted like threads; the miserable candles I still gripped in one hand pressed cruelly against my knee. I managed to spit out the canvas and gulped like a fish out of water. An orange moon floated before my eyes, then a hundred little black dots.

"Ah, it's right by your foot, Claudius," said someone.

The canvas tightened. I felt myself being lifted and then I knew nothing—for how long I cannot say. But when I regained consciousness, I was on my feet, my head free, supported by a tall man who was gripping my neck to keep me upright.

"Well now," said the man called Claudius, "he acts dizzy, don't he?"

I twisted my head.

"He wriggles," said Claudius.

"Cast off," said the other. "I'll see to him."

Claudius pushed me, and I slumped against the other man like a top run down.

"If you promise not to make a sound, I'll set you loose," said he. "Promise now!"

I nodded. I could not have spoken anyhow. My throat was parched with dust and tight with fear.

Suddenly I felt the ground move. At the same moment, I realized the three of us were standing on a small raft and that all about us was the shifting darkness of the river.

I was carelessly unwrapped like a gift no one wanted and forced to sit, my arms clasped about my knees. My captors then ignored me. They hadn't any reason to worry about my escaping. There was no place to go.

Poling the raft to keep it off the bank yet away from the swift uncertain currents, the two figures looked like pieces of the night itself. I couldn't make out their features or how they were dressed. They must be pirates, I thought, out of Barataria Bay. I had heard tales about pirates all my life but had only half believed them. Yet here I was, soon to be part of their pirate lives and pirate feasts. I shivered, feeling truly alone.

I stared at the black water and thought desperately of my father. I thought of the fate of drowned people and wondered if my father's bones lay somewhere nearby, white as chalk on the river bottom.

We were not long on the river but I wish we had been longer. The next part of our journey was on land, and I was made to walk between the two men. The marshy ground gave way beneath my feet and each time my boot sank into it, I waited with horror for a cottonmouth to strike. Sometimes there was a noisy flap of wings when we frightened a heron away from its night roost, sometimes a slither and damp muddy sigh as an otter, belly flat, headed into a pool of fetid water. We marched for several miles and although I was nearly fainting with exhaustion, I dared not ask the men to rest.

The marshy ground changed to sand. Ahead lay a stretch of water and no longer able to keep still, I asked timidly, "Is this Barataria Bay?"

"Lake Borgne," said Claudius without turning to look at me. I was given a sudden push from behind. "Keep moving," ordered the other man. "We have a long sail before us."

His words filled me with a new fear. I had by then resolved that I would somehow be able to escape from a bayou settlement of pirates, but a long sail? I nearly cried out, nearly begged them to let me go! We came to the edge of the lake and there I saw a small boat, a kind of fishing smack I'd seen on Lake Pontchartrain.

Claudius lit a lantern and held it up over my head. I looked at the two men. I could see their nostrils, their teeth like rows on an ear of corn, each hair of Claudius' black beard, pock marks, warts, scars, the very liquid of their eyes. I covered my own face, scattering bits of soft wax over my hair, all that was left of the candles for the sake of which I was surely to be killed.

My hands were snatched away and held tight.

"Don't you remember a man who gave you money?" asked one of the gaping mouths. I stared at his big face. "I'm about to do even more for you," the teeth clacked. "I'm going to take you on a fine sea voyage." He released my hands and placed an orange in them. Then I remembered his voice and his face.

It was a sailor who only that afternoon had given me two pennies to play him a martial tune down near the fruit stalls by the river. As I played, he had stuffed three oranges in his mouth, one by one, spitting out skins and pits and letting the juice run down his huge chin. It was with those pennies I had offered to buy my mother the candles she needed.

The Moonlight

I STRAINED to see the shore we were leaving and when, at last, it melted into the darkness, I was overwhelmed with sleepiness. But it is hard to settle down in the bottom of a small boat. It curved where my back didn't; I was in danger of decapitation from the wooden arm to which a sail was attached, and which swung unexpectedly from side to side. And when I thought: Here is space to stretch out in, I found I needed grasshopper legs to make room for my head, or else a turtle's neck I could pull in to make room for my legs.

I suppose I dozed now and then during that long trip. At times, the water seemed only a dense shadow which we skimmed across to avoid falling through. The men spoke in undertones about nothing familiar to me. The sail, a three-cornered patch of whiteness, swung over my head. The little boat groaned and creaked. The water tapped ceaselessly against the hull like a steady fall of rain on a roof.

Hours passed with nothing to mark them until in the east the sky paled ever so faintly as though a drop of daylight had touched the black. I wanted to stand up, to stretch. But when I started to my feet, Claudius' voice rang out so loud I was sure he would be heard on every shore. "Sit down, boy!"

We passed a small island. I saw the glimmer of a light in a win-dow—only that solitary, flickering yellow beacon. I felt hopeless and sad as though everyone in the world had died save the three of us and the unknown lamplighter on the shore. Then, as if daylight was being born inside the boat itself, I began to make out piles of rope, a wooden bucket, a heap of rusty looking net, the thick boots of my captors.

"There!" said the big-jawed man, pointing straight ahead.

And there was our destination, a sailing ship, its masts looking as high as the steeple of St. Louis Cathedral, its deck empty, a shape as astonishing on the expanse of dawn gray water as a church would have been. Across its bow were painted the words: *The Moonlight*.

I was hauled up a rope ladder from which I dared not look down, and no sooner had I reached the deck when from being so stiff and tired, I fell flat on my face. At once, my nostrils were flooded with a smell so sickening, so menacing, that it stopped my breath.

"He's not standing well," said Claudius.

"Then we must stretch him," said the other, waggling his chin.

I breathed shallowly. Despite my fatigue, I sprang to my feet and stood there quivering, my head bent back so that I faced the sky. The smell persisted but it was weaker the farther my head was from the deck. Perhaps the two men, who were tall, didn't smell it at all.

"Maybe he swims better than he stands," said Claudius.

"We'll test him in a barrel of vinegar," said the other with a broad grin. Then he placed my fife to his lips and blew mightily. His cheeks puffed out but he could make no sound.

"You haven't the gift, Purvis," said Claudius.

"Leave him be," ordered another voice, and a third man appeared from out of a little door on the deck. He was much older than my captors, and he was dressed in a thick garment that hung from his shoulders like a quilt. "Purvis, Claudius, leave him be," he repeated. "He's not going to swim away. Give him his instrument and tell him where he is."

The old man hardly glanced at me, and there was no particular kindness in his voice. Purvis, who had taken a hard grip on my wrist, dropped it.

"Thank you," I said, wishing I did not sound so timid.

"Don't waste your breath," said the old man.

"I told you you were going on a sea voyage," said Purvis.

"But I must get home!" I cried. While he spoke, I had looked around me. I had no sense of the ship at all or how one should move on it or where there was a place to lie down, the thought of which made me groan out loud.

"Now don't give up heart, boy," said Purvis. "You'll get home. Claudius and I will see to that. But it won't be for a bit."

"Oh, when!" I shouted.

"Not long at all," said Claudius softly, trying to touch my head as I ducked away from him. "With luck, you'll be back in four months."

My knees turned to pudding. "My mother will think I'm dead!" I cried, and ran wildly away from the three men only to collide with a wooden structure of some sort and knock myself to the deck where I curled up like a worm.

I thought desperately of my mother and Betty in the room with that apricot brocade. I cursed the rich stuff and the lady who had ordered a gown from my mother, and the candles I had gotten from Aunt Agatha. I cursed myself for taking the longest way home.

The old man bent over me. "You've run into my bench," he said peevishly. "Get up now and behave yourself."

I got to my feet. "It's my mother who'll be heartbroken," I said in a low voice, hoping to stir some feeling in him. "My father drowned long ago, and now she's lost me."

Purvis grabbed my arm. "We've taken care of all that, boy!" he insisted. "Claudius and me spoke to your mother and explained we'd borrowed you for a while."

I knew he was lying. But I was afraid to show him that I knew for fear he'd wrap me up in that canvas again.

"The wind's changing," Purvis muttered.

"Indeed, it's not," said the old man.

"What do you know, Ned? You can't tell whether you're on land or sea anyhow!"

"I don't require to," replied the old man sharply. Then he turned his attention back to me. "I don't approve of it," he said. "This taking of boys and men against their will. But I have nothing to do with it. We had got a boy, but he ran away in Charleston just before we sailed. Still, it isn't my fault. I'm only a carpenter. You might as well settle yourself to what's happened. The Captain will have what he will have no matter how he gets it."

"Who's on the watch?" inquired Purvis as he pressed my fife into my hand.

"Sam Wick and Cooley," answered Ned.

"I know nothing about ships," I ventured.

"You don't need to, no more than Ned here. He does his carpentering, and can even do surgery if he feels like it. But he can't tell a bowsprit from a topmast. You'll only be doing what you've done before, playing your pipe."

"For the Captain?" I asked.

Purvis opened his mouth so wide he looked like an alligator, and shouted with laughter. "No, no. Not for the Captain, but for kings and princes and other such like trash. Why, we'll have a ship full of royalty, won't we, Ned?" he said.

Misery made my head ache. I wandered away from Purvis and Ned not caring if they threw me in the water or hung me for a sail. They paid no attention to my departure but went back to quarreling about the wind.

I couldn't even feel a breeze. A gull like a puff of smoke flew across the bow. Everything except the dark smudge of shore was gray now, sky and water and dull clouds. It looked like rain. I caught my food in a coil of heavy chain, and I bumped my shoulder against a mast. Except for the mutter of Purvis' voice. I heard only the fluttering sound of water about the hull of the ship. A man passed me wearing a woolen cap, his gaze on the horizon.

There was no one to save me—and I didn't even know from what I needed to be saved. As quickly as my mother's sharp scissors cut a thread, snip! I had been cut off from the only life I knew. When I felt a hand on my arm, I supposed it was Purvis come to tease me, so I didn't turn around. But a strange voice asked, "What's your name?"

It was a plain question, asked in a plain voice. I was startled, as though life had come straight again, and turned to find a tall heavy-limbed man standing behind me. I made no reply at first. He smiled encouragingly and said, "I'm Benjamin Stout and sorry for what's been done to you."

I wanted to ask him why it had been done, but I was so grateful to be spoken to in such a sensible way that I didn't wish to provoke him. I said nothing. He leaned against the bulwark.

"How old are you? Thirteen, I'd guess. I was pressed too, although when I was older than you, and for a much longer voyage than this will be. A whole year I was gone. But then, you see, I got to like it, the sea and all, even the hard life on a ship, so that when I go ashore, I get restless in a few hours. I get half mad with restlessness. Though I promise you, there are days at sea when all you want is to be on a path that has no end, a path you can run straight ahead on till your breath gives out. Oh, I'm not speaking of gales and storms and squalls. I mean the flat dead days without wind."

"I'm thirteen," I said.

"Thirteen," he repeated thoughtfully. "Just as I said. You'll see some bad things, but if you didn't see them, they'd still be happening so you might as well."

I couldn't make sense of all that. I asked him the question that was uppermost in my mind.

"Where are we going?"

"We're sailing to Whydah in the Bight of Benin."

"Where is that?"

"Africa."

For all the calmness with which he said *Africa*, he might as well have said Royal Street. I felt like a bird caught in a room.

"You haven't told me your name," he said.

"Jessie Bollier," I replied in a whisper. For a second I was ready to throw myself off the ship. The very name of that distant place was like an arrow aimed at me.

"Jessie, we'll shake hands, now that we know each other. I'll show you to our quarters where you'll sleep. You'll get used to the hammock in a night or two. I've got so I won't sleep in anything else, and when I'm ashore, I prefer even the floor to a bed."

"Here!" roared Purvis, his heavy steps pounding toward us. "Is this boy bawling up trouble?"

"Shut your great face," Benjamin Stout called over his shoulder, then said to me, "He's harmless, only noisy. But watch out for the Mate, Nick Spark. And when you speak to the Captain, be sure and answer everything he asks you, even if you must lie."

Purvis dropped a heavy hand on my shoulder. "You've met Saint Stout, I see. Come along. Captain Cawthorne wants to see what sort of fish we caught."

His hand slid down and gripped my arm. Half dragging me, for I couldn't match his strides, he took me to a part of the ship which had a kind of small house on it, the roof forming what I later learned was the poop deck.

"Stand, Purvis," a voice ordered, as dry as paper and as sharp as vinegar. Purvis became a stone. I twitched my arm away from his grasp and rubbed it.

"Step forward, boy," said the voice. I took a step toward the two men who stood in front of the small house.

"What a fearful runt!" boomed the smaller man. Paper voice agreed, adding a high-pitched "Sir" like a sour whistle at the end of his words. I supposed from that that the short fellow was the Captain.

"Your name?" he asked.

"Jessie Bollier."

"Never heard such a name."

"It used to be Beaulieu but my father didn't want to be thought French, so he changed it," I hastened to explain, recalling Stout's advice to answer everything I was asked.

"Just as bad," said the Captain.

"Yes," I agreed.

"Captain!" roared the Captain. I jumped.

The thin man said, "Address the Captain as Captain, you boy."

"Captain," I echoed weakly.

"Purvis!" cried the Captain. "Why are you standing there, you Irish bucket! Get off to your work!"

Purvis slid away soundlessly.

"So you're one of them Creoles, are you?" asked the Captain.

"It was only my grandfather who was from France, Captain," I replied apologetically.

"Bad fellows, the French," remarked the Captain, scowling. "Pirates all of them."

"My father wasn't a pirate," I declared.

"Indeed!" sneered the Captain. He looked straight up at the sky, an odd smile on his lips. Then he coughed violently, clapped his hands together, grew silent and stared at me.

"Do you know why you are employed on this ship?"

"To play my fife for kings," I answered.

"Did you hear that, First!" the Captain cried. "That's Purvis-talk, ain't it? I'd know it anywhere. It was Purvis told you that, wasn't it?"

"Yes, Captain," I said.

"Purvis is an Irish bucket," the thin man said reflectively as though he'd only just thought of it himself.

"Well, now, listen, you miserable pygmy!"

"I will, Captain."

Without a word of warning, the little man snatched me up in his arms, held me fast to his chest and bit my right ear so hard I screamed. He set me down instantly, and I would have fallen to the deck if the thin man hadn't yanked me up by my bruised arm.

"He answers too fast, Spark," said the Captain, "but that may teach him!"

The thin man gave me a shake and let me loose, saying, "Yes, Captain, he answers much too fast."

"We are sailing to Africa," said the Captain, looking over my head, in a voice altogether different from the one with which he had been speaking. He was suddenly, insanely, calm. I wiped the blood from my neck and tried to concentrate on what he was saying.

We were sailing to Africa, the Captain repeated with a lofty gesture of his hand. And this fast little clipper would keep us safe not only from the British, but from any other misguided pirates who would try to interfere in the lucrative and God-granted trade of slaves. He, Captain Cawthorne, would purchase as many slaves as possible from the barracoon in Whydah, exchanging for them both money, $10 a head, and rum and tobacco, and returning via the island of São Tomé to Cuba where the slaves would be sold to a certain Spaniard. The ship would then return to Charleston with a hold full of molasses, and the whole voyage would take—with any luck at all—four months.

"But what is wanted is strong black youths," the Captain said excitedly, slapping Spark on his shoulder. "I wouldn't have Ibos. They're soft as melons and kill themselves if they're not watched twenty-four hours a day. I will not put up with such creatures!" Spark nodded rapidly like a chicken pecking at corn. Then the Captain scowled at me.

"You'd best learn to make yourself useful about this ship," he said. "You'd best learn every sail, for you ain't going to earn your way just by playing a few tunes to make the niggers jig!" He suddenly sighed and appeared to grow extremely dispirited. "Ah . . . you finish, Spark."

Spark finished, but what he said I'll never know. I had ceased to listen for I was thinking hard upon the one fact I'd understood. I was on a slaver.

Sometime later, Benjamin Stout showed me the quarters I was to share with the seamen. Tween decks, he called it, and you wouldn't have thought a few boys could find room in the tight airless space, much less a crew of grown men. Stout took some garments from his sea chest and handed them to me. "They'll be too big for you," he said, "but they'll do when you're soaked to the skin and need a change."

I stared up at the hammocks slung from the beams.

"You'll get used to them," Stout assured me. "Come along. I'll show you where we go for the needs of nature." I followed him to the bow of the ship. Just below was suspended a kind of platform with a grating for a floor. Two rope ends swept gently against the grating as the water shifted the ship about. "It's bad there in a heavy sea," Stout said, "but you'll get used to that, too."

"I'll not get used to anything," I replied, touching my ear now caked with dried blood.

"You have no idea how much you can get used to," said Stout.

Hungry and miserable as I was, I fell asleep in a hammock which curled about me like a peapod. I never did get entirely used to the hammock, but in time, I learned how to keep myself from falling out of it, or twisting it so I couldn't free my limbs. And although at first, upon waking, I always cracked my head against the deck above, I developed the habit of passing from deep sleep to full attention in an instant. After a few days, I had stopped clinging to the hammock like a wounded crab clings to a bit of weed.

But that first afternoon, the crack against my skull that I suffered as I sat up removed any doubts I might have had that I was dreaming. The first object my eyes rested upon was crawling idly along my leg as though I was a yard of bread. The insect was no stranger to me for we had them in all sizes at home. But I'd never thought a cockroach was a sea-going creature. I didn't care for the breed. Still, I found it a touch comforting that such a familiar land thing was making itself at home on me.

Enough light filtered through the door joints for me to see I was alone in this hole with its swaying hammocks. The smell of the place, nourished by darkness, protected against cleansing air, was terrible. I was able to distinguish sweat, soured cheese, tobacco, musty cloth and damp timbers and binding it all together, a trace of that vile smell that had forced me to my feet after I'd fallen to the deck. I heard wood creaking as though it was close to splitting. I wondered what was making my stomach so uneasy.

I brushed off the cockroach, escaped from my hammock and went up the ladder and out onto the deck. The sky was full of sunlight, and the ship's great white sails were stiffened by wind. I drew a deep breath of fresh air, which went straight to my foggy brain, and felt such a violent pang of hunger I pushed my fist against my teeth. I staggered as I moved, perhaps because I didn't know where to go, but most likely because I had never walked on the deck of a moving ship. There were several sailors near me engaged in various tasks which they didn't interrupt to even glance my way. A hand touched my shoulder. I found Ben Stout standing next to me, holding out a thick piece of bread.

"Go below to eat it," he said. "I let you sleep because you had such a harrowing night of it, but you'll be put to work soon enough."

"Thank you!" I cried gratefully, and would have spoken further with him, but he waved me away. "Don't let anyone see you eating on deck. Get below at once. I'm on the watch now. Move!"

Just before I ducked down to our quarters, I caught sight of Purvis, his hands on the helm, his feet spread wide apart, his huge face as serious as I had seen it.

I wolfed down the bread in the dark, then, unable to postpone any longer what Stout had called the needs of nature, I found my way back to that dreadful platform hanging above the water. I was so frightened, I held on to both ropes and shut my eyes tight as though by not actually *seeing* my circumstances, they would not exist. I heard a loud snort of laughter. Mortified, I opened my eyes at once to see who was observing me, for I assumed the laughter was at my expense. I looked up and saw four men, among them Purvis, leaning on the rail, their teeth bared in grins, watching me closely. I managed to gain the bow with only a scrape or two on my shins and turning my back on the jeerers, faced the shore along which we were sailing. I pretended great interest in what I saw. Soon, I grew interested in fact, for I observed that all the trees were pointing in one direction as though they'd been planted crookedly.

"Come along," Purvis said. "Stop that sulking."

When I didn't reply, he stooped over me quickly and seeing that I was gazing determinedly at the shore, he too looked in that direction.

"You'd never manage it," he said.

"I was only wondering why the trees are so bent," I said coolly.

"Prevailing wind," he answered. "Now stop being so high and mighty!"

"I suppose the ship is steering herself," I said with as much sarcasm as I could heave up at the brute.

He turned me straight about and gripped my head so I was forced to look at the helm. "My time's done," he said. "That's John Cooley who's helmsman now." Then he turned me once again.

"This is Jessie, our music man," he said to the other three seamen who stood looking at me. "And that's Isaac Porter and Louis Gardere and Seth Smith."

"Play us a tune," said Isaac Porter cheerfully.

I shook my head at which Purvis seized my sore arm and led me away. "There's some more you haven't met, not counting Cook. There's eight in the crew, excepting Cook, Ned, Spark and the Master. That means there are thirteen of us now, all because of you, so watch your step for if something goes wrong, it'll be your fault. Don't forget Jonah and what happened to him, only you shall land up in the belly of a shark—"

"Pleasanter than this . . ." I muttered.

Purvis ignored my remark. "You'll have some grub with me now," he went on. "I saw Saint Stout pass you that bread, and if I fancied I could have him flogged for that. I'm the only one beside Spark and Stout who's sailed with the Captain before, and I could tell you stories about him that would melt your ribs. A word to the wise—he likes to eat well, and he likes to beat men. The only good in him is that he's a fine seaman. Terrible, terrible with his crews, and only a little less so with the blacks. But he wants *them* in good health to make his profit. But God help the sick nigger for he'll drop him overboard between the brandy and the lighting of his pipe!"

By this time, he'd led me to a hatchway. We descended to what Purvis called the galley. There, stirring up a huge pot of lentils with a wooden ladle as though he was rowing a boat against the tide, was the thinnest man I'd ever seen. His skin was the color of suet except for uneven salmon-colored patches along the prominent ridges of his cheekbones.

"Give me my tea, Curry," demanded Purvis.

Curry slowly turned his head without ceasing his ladling, and gave Purvis such a furious look that I expected him to attack him physically. Purvis nicked my neck with his finger and announced, as if Curry was deaf, "Cooks are all like him, though Curry is worse than some. It's the smoke that maddens them, and whatever good humor they start with is fried to a crisp by the heat."

Curry suddenly abandoned his ladle, darted about a minute or two, then slammed a bowl of tea in front of Purvis, and a square biscuit that banged on the table like a stone. Purvis took a filthy rag from under his shirt, wrapped it around the biscuit, then let his fist fall upon it like a hammer.

"I should like to find out who makes these things," he said pensively, as his fist fell, "for I would do the same to them as I am doing to this biscuit."

He rose and hunted about in the greasy dark smoke that surrounded Curry like a cloak, returning with something in his hand which he tossed at me. It was the driest curl of sorry looking meat I'd ever seen. Then he pushed his bowl of tea toward me. "Take a bite of the beef, then a swig of tea. Hold them both in your mouth until the beef softens."

As I sat there on the narrow little bench, breathing in the close clay-like smell of lentils, and drinking tea from Purvis' bowl, I felt almost happy. When I remembered the wretchedness of my situation, I wondered if there was something about a ship that makes men glide from one state of mind to another as effortlessly as the ship cuts through water.

John Cooley and Sam Wick were the last members of the crew I met. Cooley did not even glance at me, and Wick laughed foolishly and observed that my feet were too large for the rest of me. I joined Purvis on the bench he'd brought from some place below, and I watched him mending a sail. "Sews like a lady," shouted Claudius Sharkey as he passed us by.

Porter and Wick and Sharkey were topmen, Purvis told me, responsible for the masts, while the rest of the crew worked the lower sails and took turns at the wheel. As for him, he said proudly, he was a sailman, and knew all there was to know about sails which was "as good as knowing the gospel straight through, and takes a lot more thought."

I was still afraid of Purvis, for I thought him as unpredictable in his moods as a frog is in the direction of its jumps. In some ways, Purvis resembled a very large frog. But he seemed to have taken a sort of fondness for me, and that evening, I learned a good deal my eyes alone could not have taught me.

Purvis was never idle, nor were the other sailors unless they'd just come off watch. I saw that day, and didn't forget, that a ship must be tended to day and night as though it was the very air one took into one's lungs, and that to neglect it for a second was to risk dangers which, at that time, I could only imagine when Purvis recounted tales of storms at sea, masts split like twigs, crews swept overboard by giant waves, men caught in flying anchor cables and flung, broken, into the churning water. There was no way to leave off the work of a ship.

I hadn't noticed the man way up near the top of a mast until Purvis pointed him out.

"There's always someone stationed on the foretop sailyard," he said. "And if a sail appears, the Captain must look through his spyglass to make sure what it is."

Then he spoke of pirating, especially in the waters near the islands of the West Indies. When I asked him why Captain Cawthorne had spoken of the British he looked both sly and angry.

"They're worse than the pirates, Jessie!" he cried. "Why, they try to board our ships as if we still belonged to them. But there's laws against that, and those laws give us the right to sink them if they try anything. Oh, but they do make trouble for us, blockading the African coast, and sniffing about Cuba."

"But why?" I asked.

"They've different laws than us. They've entirely stopped the slave trade in their own country—the worse for them—and would like us to copy them in their folly. Why, the trade is the best trade there is! Black Gold, we call it! Still, there's one way they help us. The native chiefs are so greedy for our trade goods, they sell their people cheaper than they ever did to tempt us to run the British blockade. So we profit despite the damned Englishmen."

Later, he spoke of the arms *The Moonlight* carried, but gave me no details of them, nor would he explain what he meant when he mentioned flags from various countries which the Captain kept in his quarters.

At first the wind had been a tight fist, shoving us on, but now it was an open hand pushing us before it at such a rousing clip I felt my own arms had become wings as we flew across the water. Ben Stout called out to me that the ship was *speaking*. He pointed down at the wake that purled and foamed behind us as though a razor had slit the dark surface of the sea and allowed its mysterious light to shine through.

I had often noticed the gait of sailors about the river front in New Orleans, and understood it better now as I made my way about the ship. Although our progress was smooth that day, one of my legs always felt shorter than the other. You had to keep a kind of balance as though you were walking along the back of a cantering horse.

Except for Purvis and Ben Stout, the rest of the crew barely noticed me. They did not speak much among themselves, going about their work in a hard relentless fashion.

Ben Stout showed me a wooden pin that fitted into a hole in the rail. It had several purposes, he explained, one of which was to make fast a rope by winding it on a cleat, another, to knock an unruly seaman on his head, and still another, to kill rats. This last concerned me. Rat hunts were part of the ship's routine, he said. They'd eat up everything if they weren't kept down. I must learn to seek them out, kill them and toss them overboard.

There were other crawling and creeping things, beetles and worms and such like, but they were as much a part of a ship as its timbers and, he said, could be killed for pleasure, not out of necessity. He removed a hatch cover and showed me the hold where the drinking water was stored in wooden casks. "You'll have to be spry to run after the rats down there," he said. "They're as smart as the Devil himself."

"And if I'm bit?" I asked, pretending by my tone I was only making a joke.

"Bite them back," he replied. "And when it rains, you'll help set out the casks for fresh water. The worms and the beetles can make off with our stores—we can survive a storm with broken masts, but without water, we're a dead ship."

He told me then that we must all share one bucket of water a day for our washing, and the longer the voyage took, the less drinking water we would be given. "The Mate doles it out once a day, not a drop more than the Captain allows."

"And does the Captain get rationed too?"

Ben snorted. "The Captain of this ship would drink your blood before he'd go without. Haven't you noticed his chicken coops? The boxes of vegetables he's got growing there aft?" I shook my head. I had no wish to go near the Captain. My ear was still sore. Ben gestured at the hold.

"That's where the slaves will be stowed," he said, "right on those casks, and in the aft hold when we've unloaded the rum."

"But there's not room for a dozen men!" I exclaimed.

"Captain Cawthorne's a tight packer," Ben said.

"I'm what!" roared a voice.

We turned from the hold to discover Cawthorne himself standing not two feet away.

"Sir," said Stout smartly. "I was explaining his work to the boy."

"Were you indeed? I thought you was describing *my* work to Bollweevil here. That's your name, ain't it, lad? Yes. I'm a tight packer, as neat as a pin, stack them up like flannel cakes, one top of the other. Ah—it's the British who've forced me to be so ingenious, Bollweevil, for we must have speed before all else, and speed means a ship without the comforts, stripped down, a ship like a winged serpent. You see—?" he held out his arms, and I ducked, thinking he meant to mark my other ear, but he dropped them to his sides almost at once, shook his head, and muttering something about studding sails, stomped off aft.

I sighed mightily.

Ben Stout said, "You can't never tell about him . . ."

He was about to replace the hatch cover, when, perhaps because of some slight change of wind, I caught a powerful whiff of that ugly smell mixed with something else. I sniffed, thinking to myself what a comical human habit it was—how often I'd observed someone who, offended by an odor and proclaiming loudly how awful it was, continued to sniff away as though, in fact, he was smelling a rose.

"That's chloride of lime," Ben said.

"What's that?"

"What we sprinkled in the hold after our last cargo of slaves was unloaded."

"Why?"

Ben put his foot on the hatch. "To clear out the stench. But it never quite goes away."

I felt a thrill of fear as if a bottle had crashed next to me, and the bits of glass were flying toward my face. I asked him nothing more.

Claudius Sharkey was at the helm and he let me look at the ship's compass. It seemed to me to be the finest looking thing aboard although I understood it no better than I did the time divisions marked by the ship's bell.

Curry had made a spice duff for our supper. I amused myself by amassing as many raisins as I could before Purvis snatched them up and thrust them in his big mouth, grinning at me and chewing at the same time. I wanted to stay and watch Curry knead the flour paste in his kneading trough, but Stout ordered me to get below and to my hammock.

I felt the ship's movement in my very bones as I lay there, rocking back and forth. I thought of the rigging, the yards, the ratlines up which I'd seen the seamen move as easily as though they'd been walking on level ground, and I hoped I'd never have to set foot on those precarious spider webs. The ratlines began to blur and extend into a wake of rope as sleepiness overcame me. Suddenly I heard a great shout. I peered over the edge of my hammock.

There was Purvis sitting on a sea chest, drinking from a mug.

" 'And I'll have none of that,' he says. 'And I'll have some of that,' she says. 'And we'll none of us have none of that,' we say," he roared. Then he grew silent and peered up at my face. By the weak light of the oil lamp, I saw a benign smile stretch his big mouth.

"Did you hear something, Jessie, lad?" he asked gravely.

"Why, yes," I replied. "I heard you shouting about some of this and some of that."

"You're mad!" He cried, rising to his feet. "There wasn't nobody here but me, and I was only quietly drinking my little tot of warm wine."

I fell back, breathing as softly as I could, praying he'd forget I was there.

It began again—" 'and we'll none of us have none of that,' we say . . ."

Silence.

"Did you hear anything, lad?" asked Purvis in a wheedling voice.

"No, sir, nothing at all!" I replied hastily.

"Then you're deaf as a post!" he exclaimed, and clapped his hand against the bottom of my hammock with considerable force.

I lay motionless, my hands over my mouth to muffle my laughter. Once I let it out, I knew I'd not be able to stop, such had been my fear, such was now my relief.

The Shrouds

THE TRUTH CAME SLOWLY like a story told by people interrupting each other. I was on a ship engaged in an illegal venture, and Captain Cawthorne was no better than a pirate.

At first, these hard facts had been clouded over by the crew's protestations that the sheer number of ships devoted to the buying and selling of Africans was so great that it cancelled out American laws against the trade—"nothing but idle legal chatter," Stout remarked, "to keep the damned Quakers from sermonizing the whole country to death!"

All the crew protested, that is, except Ned Grime the carpenter, who talked as if he lived a mile from the earth and had nothing to do with the idiot carryings on of the human race. But when I discovered that Ned, too, like all the rest of the men, held a share of the profit to be realized from the sale of the blacks, I paid little attention to his pretense of aloofness.

It was Sharkey who told me that not only the British cruisers made the slave trade hazardous. United States Revenue Cutters patrolled our own shores after privateers, and the smugglers who landed small groups of blacks in Georgia and Florida. I learned then that there were American laws, too, against the importing of slaves. He spread his hands as wide as he could to show me the money the smugglers made after they'd taken the slaves inland and sold them at the slave markets in the larger southern cities.

Those first days, the weather was splendid and we sometimes made a speed of 14 knots. Captain Cawthorne rolled about the deck, hilarious and noisy, hitting members of the crew out of sheer high spirits. Once I saw him do a strange little dance on the poop deck, holding up the skirt of his jacket and kicking out his legs.

"Pray the weather holds," Stout said to me. "The Captain's so stubborn he won't take in sail no matter how fierce the wind—not so long as he can see the bowsprit!"

My days were full. I was everybody's boy. But I had time to myself now and then, a moment when I was not fetching the Captain his tea and rum, or heaving waste over the side, or learning to mend a sail while Purvis howled at my clumsy fingers, or tracking the rats which, not content with the foods stores, would gnaw ropes and sail if not caught. Then I would find myself a corner on the deck and stare at the sea, or the distant coastline of Florida which we followed until we passed through the straits which separated it from Cuba.

How strange it was to see another ship! A taut sail in the distance like an unknown word written across the vast expanse of sky; a ship carrying a crew like *The Moonlight*'s and perhaps someone like me.

There was no getting used to it for me—living the ordinary life of an eating and sleeping creature but on a thing that always moved, a wooden thing whose fate could be changed by a shift of wind, a sudden piling up of briny water, by currents and rain.

One morning I told Ned my thoughts.

"The earth itself moves," he said in his chilly way.

"That may be," I replied. "But I don't feel it."

"Why should you!" the old man snapped. "God has no wish to share his secrets with Adam's descendants." He loosened the vise around a piece of wood he was smoothing. He looked straight up at the heavens. "Once there was a garden where all was known," he said in an odd dreamy way.

My sister, Betty, had once embroidered a piece of linen with a bright blue sea and a little brown boat like a pecan. But the sea was not only blue. Sometimes it was a color that was like the smell of salt wind. And at the end of the day, the sun could stain the water yellow as cane stalks, green as limes, pink and orange as shrimps.

I did not brood upon them much, my mother and Betty. They had sunk quietly to a place in the back of my mind. When I did picture them, they moved silently about, doing the things I had seen them do all my life, sewing and cleaning, washing and eating, going to market. It was only now and then I would feel a sharp thrust of pain and worry when I told myself that they must think me dead.

Once, during a rain squall, while the sea groaned about us, bearing upon its heaving back great forks of lightning, I wished most desperately to be off this ship, to be anywhere but on it. A kind of breathlessness shut my throat. I thought I was choking to death. It was Purvis who picked me up and shook me as I began to sob with terror. He hit me about the shoulders. If I didn't stop, he shouted, he'd have me up in the shrouds where I'd get more than air in my lungs.

That night, I lay in my hammock, a sorry thing soaked through to its bones. All the batches had been closed against the rain. The smell of wet wool stuffed my nostrils, the pickled cabbage I had had for my midday meal seemed to have re-formed itself in my stomach, and finally the thick mumble of complaint from Sharkey and Isaac Porter, who were always arguing, drove me up on deck.

The rain had abated. We were moving like an arrow, like a sky ship, among the points of light which were stars.

I knew it must be Purvis on the watch, for while I was idly counting stars, a great wad of vile brown stuff flew by my ear as he expelled his gob of chewing tobacco over the side. I ducked and heard a dark chuckle, its human familiarity overcoming the sound of the speaking ship, the creaking masts, the great thunk and slap of the sails, the breathing sea.

Perhaps the night and the sea leads a person to thoughts of his life. It did me. I thought about how the only grown people I had really known up to now were women—I wouldn't count the parson, who was a stick notched with pious sayings, or the doctor at Charity Hospital who treated my sister with tonics and ointments—and here there were no females save the Captain's hens. I had not known that among men there were such differences. That thought led me to wonder why I didn't like Benjamin Stout. I surprised myself. I hadn't known till that second that *liking* mattered—what had mattered before was how I was treated. And Stout treated me kindly, showing me things the rest of the crew wouldn't have troubled themselves with, getting me extra helpings of rice and beef while Curry had his back turned, steaming away his brains over his cook stove.

But it was Purvis whom I was eager to see when I awoke in the morning. Purvis, with his horrible coarse jokes, his bawling and cursing, Purvis, whom I trusted.

The Captain had settled on the name Bollweevil, and I winced when I heard him call it out. Some of the crew had taken it up but when they used it, I turned my back. The Captain was still cheerful; I listened to him sing out his commands while the wind held fair. I learned some of the words of his song but had great difficulty connecting them up with the lengths of canvas to which they applied. Purvis said a sailor must know every sheet and brail and halyard so that on the darkest night he wouldn't make an error which could cost the life of the ship and the crew. I especially liked the words, skysail and moonsail, and turned them over in my mouth as though I was licking honey. But the sailing of the ship was something so far beyond my powers of understanding that I didn't trouble my mind about it. Although I found most of the crew rough men who were often cruel, I could not help but admire the fearless way they swarmed up the ratlines and hung over the yards as sure of their perch as birds on a limb.

As for the Mate, Nicholas Spark, against whom Stout had warned me, I had little to do with him. He kept to the Captain's side like a shadow. He had a brooding look on his face, and when he spoke, his voice sizzled like a hot poker plunged into water.

We had been at sea now for nearly three weeks when one morning after the deck had been holystoned, the wind dropped entirely. No one appeared surprised except me. But then I knew nothing of the sky and how to read its signs.

For several days, *The Moonlight* made little progress, and that little because of a brief fierce blow that strained every sail. Certain changes had been taking place aboard which I had barely noticed, but the becalming of the ship brought my attention back to it. Gratings had replaced the solid hatches over the holds. A huge cauldron had appeared in Curry's galley, and one morning I found John Cooley working intently on an object which, though I'd never seen one before, made me shiver.

It was a whip with nine knotted cords. As I approached, he began to fasten the cords to a handle. I didn't want to look at it. But I couldn't keep my eyes from it. Cooley looked up. Our eyes met. He laughed.

I turned away and discovered Spark staring at me from the helm. Cooley laughed again. A sail flapped somewhere nearby. Spark's frozen glare never wavered. The sun seemed impaled by the mizzenmast. I felt hot and cold. Then Purvis slouched by, calling over his shoulder, "Jessie, I'll put a hitch in your arm if you don't get below and catch up with the rats! They're about to overtake us, boy."

The moment passed. When I glanced back at Spark he was saying something to the helmsman, and Cooley was getting to his feet. Just before I dropped down into the hold, I saw Cooley flick the whip and nod to himself.

The ship was going nowhere under a sky that darkened into a windless night and lightened into a day so motionless, so empty, we were like a plate poised on the edge of a pit without bottom. The

Captain and the Mate roamed the deck, their eyes on the sky, and the seamen quarreled.

They quarreled from morning until night and in the middle of the night. Benjamin Stout lost his smile when he found his sea chest emptied, and all its contents strewn about, his razor and strop, his knife and fork, his sheath knife and the fid he used for splicing, and his small seaman's Bible, its pages damp as though it'd been dipped in brine.

During those days, a fever seemed to pass among us, leaving everyone weak yet restless. Stout accused Purvis of emptying out his sea chest. He seemed to think it the worst of a list of crimes of which he accused Purvis. Purvis swore and threw his ham fists in the air. The others added fuel to the fire, inciting them both to what end I don't know. I stayed out of our quarters as often as I could and once slept on the deck where Spark, finding me huddled near the bow, gave me a terrible kick that sent me rolling.

It was that dawn when the light was the color of the sea itself, and I could hardly make out the line of the horizon, that I saw a figure, its head wrapped in cloth so I couldn't recognize it, moving furtively on all fours toward the aft section. Although I was afraid Nick Spark would return, I was so curious about the creeping man that I stayed where I was.

I searched the deck with my eyes but either the Mate had evaporated or gone to his quarters. If Gardere and Seth Smith, who passed within a foot of where I was crouched near the ship's small boat, had seen the creeper, they didn't, apparently, care to investigate.

Not five minutes later, along the same route, like a sightless worm that must go by smell, the creeper returned. But this time, it crawled along on only three limbs for one hand was held up, its begrimed fingers holding a beautiful white egg which, in that dim light, was as luminous as a tiny moon rising between deck and rail.

The air was damp and sea-soaked, and I breathed it in as though it were a draught of fresh water. But no sooner did I imagine what it would be like to drink up a whole pond than I skittered away from the thought. Our water ration had been cut. The longer it would take to reach our destination, the less we would have. God knows my family was poor! But there wasn't an end to anything. We'd always had something to eat and drink. For the first time in my life, I could, if I put my mind to it, see to the end of a thing needed for life to go on.

We lived off what our ship could carry, but the ship drank the wind, and without that, ship and crew would be lost in the wastes of the ocean.

I made haste to return below. There, I found Purvis, Stout and Sharkey looking at the egg, an ordinary enough object in the light of the oil lamp. Someone had placed it in a tarpaulin hat, and the three sailors stared down at it as though it was a priceless jewel.

Although we'd had no eggs for our mess, I thought they were making a bit much of it. Still frightened by my vision of empty water casks, I said, "Would Curry give me some beer, do you think?" hoping one of the men would answer.

Stout murmured, "Don't fret, lad. I'll see you get what you need." But Purvis let go of the hat, leaving it in Stout's hands, and gave me a wallop across my back.

"None of that mewling," he said furiously. "None of us is better off save two we won't mention, and I'll have no cat cries from you, Jessie. You get the same amount to drink as all of us, and that's a far sight better than you'd do on some ships I can think of."

I shrugged as coolly as I could, but felt better, not that I would have admitted it to Purvis.

Despite the murky dawn, the morning was clear and sunny. Later that day, a wind of sorts blew up. At the first breath of it, the men straightened their backs and moved smartly about the deck. Their voices rang out clearly, and in the galley, Curry sang a tune to himself in a horrible cracked voice that sounded as if it had been fried in lard. Only Nicholas Spark stalked about the ship like a spirit of mold and decay.

We made good speed that day, although as dusk approached the wind slackened somewhat, as did our spirits. Then we were summoned to the deck, even those men who were resting after their watch.

We stood in a clump amidships while all about us a great flaring sky of twilight burnished our faces and streaked the masts with a tender golden light.

The Captain and Spark were some distance away from us, regarding us fixedly. Gardere was at the helm, and Sam Wick and Smith were occupied with the sails. The eerie silence, the molten hills of the sea, the unmoving figures of Master and Mate filled me with dread and yet a kind of exhilaration as though we were all waiting for the appearance of something supernatural. Then the Captain spoke.

"It has come to my attention—I'll not confide to you how—that a certain precious thing has been taken from me, stole in the dark by a scoundrel, grasped by his filthy claws, made off with to his hole." He paused. In the awesome silence that followed his words, I saw once again that dawn apparition carrying the moon egg.

"To its hole!" the Captain's voice rang out. "And there, EATEN!" he screamed. "My precious thing, EATEN!"

Spark stepped forward holding in his hands a length of tarred rope.

"That scoundrel, that Irish bucket, that thieving scum of the earth, will now show himself," the Captain ordered, his voice suddenly quiet.

None of us moved.

"Purvis!" cried Spark in his burnt out voice. "Forward, Purvis!"

Purvis went to stand before them.

"The wind's freshening again, ain't it?" the Captain observed conversationally to Spark.

"I believe it is, Sir," replied the Mate.

"It'll blow hard this night, would you say, Spark?"

"I would, Sir."

"Cooley, Stout, fasten the egg-stealing serpent to the mast," said the Captain.

Without a second's hesitation, the two sailors took hold of Purvis and bound him with ropes to the mast.

"Now, Spark, remove his shirt with your rope!" ordered the Captain.

Nicholas Spark flogged Purvis' shirt from his back. Beneath the leaping of the rope, blood and cloth mixed. The sun began to die on the horizon, and still he beat him. Faint, my legs like porridge, I leaned against Ned who made not the slightest accommodation of his body to my weight. I wept silently. Purvis groaned and moaned but never cried out.

At what seemed to be the last fading ray of sun, the tarred rope fell from the Mate's hand. He turned to the Captain, his face as smooth as the surface of a stone.

"Now tie him to the shrouds," said the Captain. "The air will refresh his corrupt soul."

I barely slept that night. Once, I peeped out at the deck. Far above, like a huge tattered bird, its wings flapping, hung Purvis, tied to the shrouds where the wind beat against him as though animated by the same demon which had raised Nicholas Spark's arm and brought the tarred rope down on his back.

Toward morning, I overheard a conversation.

Smith said, "You handed Purvis over to that beast."

"He would have done the same in my place," said Stout.

"You're a damned foul creature, Stout."

"No different from you or anyone else," Stout said mildly from his hammock.

"You're one with Cawthorne," Smith said. "No difference between you except he's ambitious."

"That may be true, Seth," said Stout. "I wish I had Cawthorne's ambition. I would have made a fine rich man," and he laughed.

Then I heard Ned asking who had informed on Purvis.

"Why, I wouldn't be surprised if it was Stout himself," said Seth Smith.

"No, no. I didn't do that," said Stout. "I expect Spark saw me. But then, you see," he continued amiably as though discussing the best way to splice a rope, "Purvis and me has sailed with the Captain and Spark before, and I believe they favor me a bit over him."

It was more than I could take in. My head felt swollen and my cheeks on fire.

Why hadn't Purvis denied the theft of the egg? I couldn't find a word to put to Stout's actions. Why didn't the rest of the men seize him and toss him overboard? Why didn't they go to the Captain and inform him of the real culprit? Why was Stout so calm, even satisfied as he lay there in the damp dark, accused of dreadful treachery by a fellow sailor, unmoved, unashamed, and now as I could hear plainly, snoring contentedly?

Sharkey and Smith brought Purvis down in the morning. Ned took a bottle of salve from his medicine chest and rubbed it into the wounds on Purvis' back as he sat hunched over on his sea chest. I brought him a mug of tea and rum and he drank it down slowly, his face creased like rumpled parchment, as white as though the wind had blown the blood out of him. He looked at me over the rim of the mug. His eyes had sunk into his head.

We were alone for a few minutes. I stood looking at him, unable to tear my gaze away. He groaned softly now and then, or shook his big head as though something was flying about in his hair and bothering him. Then he let the mug fall into my hands.

"I'll be all right soon, Jessie," he said in a cracked thin voice.

"But—it was Stout!" I cried.

"Oh, yes. It was Stout."

"But why didn't you say?" I pleaded, beside myself with rage at the injustice.

"There would've been no use in that. The officers of this ship would not care what the truth was. Get me a plug of tobacco, will you, Jessie? It'll make me feel human."

I fetched it for him. With great effort, he broke off a piece and stuck it in his mouth. "Ah . . ." he sighed.

"But if it wasn't you—" I began.

"The Captain had it in his mind that it was time for a flogging—to remind the men."

"To remind the men? Of what?" I demanded.

Purvis clasped his hands and leaned further forward.

"No more talk now, Jessie. I'll rest," he said.

Stout handed me a piece of cheese that morning as I sat near Ned's bench sewing a piece of canvas. I took it and heaved it over the side.

Stout smiled gently as though he couldn't blame me.

The Bight of Benin

NED THE CARPENTER had been unusually busy. The result of his labor was a platform on which squatted a nine-pound carronade, black as a bat, absorbing sunlight or the white glare of sunless days, an iron presence which Nicholas Spark touched each time he passed it as though for luck.

I didn't need Purvis to tell me we were soon to meet up with other men. The armament was enough.

An American flag on the signal gaff would discourage the British from boarding us. The carronade would warn them we belonged to ourselves. Purvis had heard there was some kind of American warship that was supposed to prevent the trade, but with thousands of miles of coast to patrol, there was small chance we'd meet up with it. "Besides," he said, "there is the matter of the flags."

"What flags?" I asked.

"The flags in the Captain's quarters," Purvis said. "It's this way, Jessie. If an American patrol should signal us and demand to board the ship, we'd run up a Spanish flag. And if they persisted, we'd show them a full set of papers that would prove *The Moonlight* to be of Spanish ownership."

"But anyone could tell we're not!"

"I tell you, such things are decided by papers!" Purvis declared. "If the papers are in order, nothing else matters. It works both ways. The Spanish slavers hire an American citizen to take passage with them. Then, if they're boarded by the British, the American puts on a captain's hat, takes command of the ship, flourishes his ownership papers and threatens to sue the British naval officer who's dared to set foot on his deck! There's not so many willing to risk the penalty for boarding a ship and finding neither slaves nor equipment on it. I sailed once under a master who, though he grew rich from slaving, wasn't caught for ten years. When he was finally boarded at the mouth of the Volta

River, he was dropping slaves over the port side of the ship while his Portuguese servant was dressed up in captain's clothes, cursing the British as they scrambled up the starboard side. They couldn't prove a thing against him!"

"But there are many against the trade," I said, irritated that Purvis was so satisfied with his arguments.

"Oh, Jessie! Don't you see? The British like to provoke us because we don't belong to them any more!"

"But they've outlawed slavery in their own country!"

Purvis stroked his chin and narrowed his eyes. "You can be sure," he said with conviction, "that they wouldn't have passed laws against slaving if they hadn't found something else as profitable. That's the way of things, Jessie. But you'll see! You're bound to get a bit of a share yourself at the end of this voyage!"

I felt the force of truth withheld and hidden behind Purvis' grin and so, perhaps to remind him of an event that he couldn't so easily smooth out and explain as British law, I asked, "Does your back still pain you?"

He scowled and threw out his fist.

"Never mind that!" he growled.

I crawled into my hammock with much on my mind.

Life had turned upside down. My friend was a man who'd press-ganged me. I disliked the man who'd befriended me. For all that talk of papers, I could see clear enough that two governments were against this enterprise, even though my own was, according to Purvis, weak in its opposition. Purvis had said the native kings sold their own people willingly, yet he'd also told me there were chiefs who would sink the ship and kill us all if they had the chance.

"Play us a tune," Purvis' voice floated up to me with a certain melancholy note. "We haven't had a tune from you all these weeks, and soon enough you'll be playing, but not for us."

I peered over the edge of the hammock. Smith and Purvis were looking up at me expectantly. I took my fife and jumped down and played as fast and loud as I could. The two men danced in the small space, circling each other like two dreaming bears, their faces as serious as though they were reading from the Bible.

We entered the Bight of Benin at midday. By nightfall, we were off Whydah. There, I heard the cable strike the deck as the anchor rushed downwards, hooking us to that whole unknown land greeted earlier by Sharkey from his foretop lookout with a shout of, "Land, ho . . ."

I looked eagerly toward the shore as though with a glance I could take in the feel of solid earth, the comfort of it, after all these days on the rolling back of the sea.

But the land was on fire. Sheets of flame as red and jagged as the wounds the rope had opened in Purvis' back flew upward into a darkening sky. Clouds of smoke mixed with low-lying rain clouds. It seemed as though a great forest was dying.

"It's the barracoon," remarked Seth Smith, who had come to stand beside me at the taffrail. "The British devils have set it afire."

"Barracoon?" I asked, but Smith rushed on impatiently. "The British, the British!" he cried. "They've set the barracoon on fire, and the damned niggers that have been held for us have run off and escaped!"

I asked him what a barracoon was.

"That's a confined place where the chiefs keep them chained and ready for trade. And the British, who pretend that they own the entire world, sneak ashore, let them loose and destroy property that ain't theirs."

"Then we won't be trading—with the slaves all gone?"

He laughed loudly. "The slaves are *never* gone!" he exclaimed. "All of Africa is nothing but a bottomless sack of blacks."

"Will we land soon?"

"*We* won't never land," he said angrily as though I'd been impertinent. "It's the Captain who takes samples of our rum to the chiefs. He'll go at night in the small boat and leave Spark to see to the ship and us. Now look over there! You see those ships?" he asked. "That's some of the British Squadron, waiting to pounce. They've done their day's nasty work on shore, and now they'll rub their hands at the thought of this tasty little ship coming all this way only to have to sit and wait."

"They know what we're here for?"

"Lord! Of course, they know. They've had a glass on us since we entered the Bight. It's cat and mouse now. But Cawthorne will do it. He's a fierce man."

I looked away from the distant cluster of ships, back at the enormous fan of fire. Only through Purvis' stories had I been able to imagine the destructive power of the sea. Our voyage had been, except for a few days of calm and a squall or two, without special incident. But I knew the horror of fire. Only three years ago, 107 houses had been eaten up by flames in New Orleans, and the smell of charred wood, the smoke, the fire that ran where it would, had frightened me so much that for many weeks I would not sit near the candles in our room. When they were lit at night, and I stared into the little eye of the flame, I would see myself running through molten lakes like those our parson described when he shouted at us about the hell awaiting sinners.

"He'll go up and down the coast here," Smith continued challengingly as though daring the distant British ships and their crews. "Yes, he will! And along with the rum, he'll carry the shackles the chiefs will require for the slaves. Then, one night, there'll come to our ship a long canoe filled to the brim with blacks—and the next night, another canoe, so quiet, you won't know it's alongside until the slaves are on deck, wailing and weeping and biting their own flesh. They're all mad, the blacks! And the British will sweat with rage, for they have no right to search us. The only danger for us is if the British are able to notify the American patrol. But I tell you, such a ship is only here to protect us against any abuse by the damned English! For as everyone knows, our whole country is for the trade, in spite of the scoundrels who cry and fling themselves about at the fate of the *poor poor* black fellows. Poor indeed! Living in savagery and ignorance. Think on this—their own chiefs can't wait to throw them in our holds!"

"But what can the British do?"

"They could try to blockade us if we were so unwise as to sail up a river. They could force us, once we've taken on slaves and unloaded our cargo, to put on so much sail we'd be in danger if they gave chase."

"You've been on slavers before," I said.

"All of us have," he replied. "It's nasty work. And it's not everyone has the nerve for it." His mood suddenly changed for he gave me a big grin. "Perhaps you'll be carrying a pistol yourself, runt that you are!"

"A pistol!"

"Aye. We're all armed as long as we're in sight of the coast. If the blacks try anything, it'll be then, when they can still see where they came from. Oh, they've done terrible things I could tell you about! Killing a crew and a master and all, then flinging themselves back into the sea, even shackled!"

I thought suddenly of the stories I had heard at home about slave uprisings in Virginia and South Carolina. My breath came short—here, within eyesight, was the very world from which such slaves had been taken. Here, on this small ship, we would be carrying God knows how many of them, and I, without at this instant being able to conceive in what manner, was to make them dance.

"Why must the slaves dance?" I asked timidly, for fear of annoying Smith. At that moment, I was afraid of everyone on *The Moonlight*, just as I had been when I first set my foot upon her deck.

"Because it keeps them healthy," said Smith. "It's hard to make a profit out of a sick nigger—the insurance ain't so easy to collect. And it makes any Captain wild to jettison the sick ones within sight of the marketplace itself after all the trouble he's gone to."

Smith went off and left me to my apprehension. It didn't let up much until the next dawn when I saw land clearly for the first time.

Green and brown and white, trees and shore and waves. I thought of home. At the same time, I was overcome by a dreadful thirst.

I thought I had grown accustomed to doing without everything that was familiar, accepting small rations of water and food without question. But the sight of the land, a longing to set foot on something that didn't rock and pitch and groan and creak, made the room on Pirate's Alley the only place in the world I wanted to be. To sit on a bench there in a private patch of sunlight and slowly peel and eat an orange! At that moment, I glimpsed Purvis dragging an enormous tarpaulin across the deck.

I hated him!

"Give me a hand with this, Jessie," he shouted. I didn't move.

"Just take up the end of it," he called again.

Still, I remained unmoving, nearly senseless with rage.

"Get to it!" said the awful dead voice of Nicholas Spark.

Not for the last time, I considered casting myself over the side and confounding them all! But I submitted, convinced there was no one on the ship who would throw me a rope and rescue me from the water. I went slowly toward Purvis, feeling a shame I'd never felt before.

With my help and Gardere's, Purvis set up a tent on the deck. He volunteered the information that it was for the slaves to sit under when they had their meals. I had not inquired, and I made no comment. I wasn't much better off than the slaves would be, I told myself. I felt utterly alone among the men now. I couldn't even smile at Curry's peculiar mutterings as he went rooting about in his galley, cooking up the foul messes which I would have to eat or else starve.

Benjamin Stout, who had not ceased to speak kindly to me despite the cold way I behaved toward him, followed me around asking why I was wearing such a scowl.

"Leave me be!" I cried at him finally, after he'd tracked me right to my hammock.

"If he speaks to someone, it won't be to an egg stealing cockroach like yourself, Ben Stout," said Purvis, his head hanging above the ladder to our quarters like a moon that's been roundly punched. "It won't be a man who lets his shipmate hang in the shrouds for him."

"He's in such a dark mood," Stout remarked in a pleasant tone as though he were conversing with a friend. "I was only worried what was bothering the boy."

Stout was surely the worst creature I'd ever known or heard about, worse even then Nicholas Spark.

"Worried," jeered Purvis. "You, worried! It's only that evil curiosity of yours that makes you want to poke and pry and fiddle! Jessie, come up on deck. Come on now! There's a good boy! Don't sulk so! It makes us all worried, to be near the shore like this and not able to walk on it. But think, the voyage is half over. You'll be home, if the trade winds are good to us, in just this time again. And richer too!" I didn't move. "Well, if you won't speak, I can't hang here like a ham for smoking."

Ham. Oh, ham! And a cask of water!

I stayed for a long time below, and I was left alone. Perhaps Purvis took pity on me and saw to it that I was not sent for. I softened a little in my feeling toward him partly because he'd spoken my very thoughts about the land teasing me there, so close, so out of reach.

Time hung on us. Three days we sat there like a wooden bird. The sky threatened rain but rain never fell. Sharkey got into the rum and staggered about the deck shouting and cursing until Spark laid him flat with a belaying pin. The blood ran from the wound, then dried. I stared at his head with a hard heart. No one should have the advantage of me any more. I cast a murderous look at Spark's back. I kicked the mast and cursed. No one took notice.

The great cauldron I'd seen Curry scrubbing was brought up on deck. The Captain called all hands together and handed out pistols, but not to me or Purvis.

"Not you, you serpent," he said to Purvis. "You might put a bullet through the head of my last hen." He said nothing to me.

There were more than Sharkey who got into the rum. At night, the ship rang with snatches of blurred song, of shouted angry words, of broken silly laughter, and sometimes, of blows given and taken. Only Ned and Ben Stout stayed sober, Ned observing the goings-on with an indifferent eye, Ben, reading his small Bible by oil lamp with an aggrieved but forgiving look on his face. Once he assured me not to fear his mates. I hadn't asked him for any assurance and told him so.

On the fourth night, the Captain came aboard from wherever he'd been, followed by a tall thin coffee-colored man.

Purvis and I watched them go into the Captain's quarters. "That's the *cabociero*," said Purvis. "He's a Portuguese black, what you could call a broker. The Captain must pay him a tax for our anchorage here. Then they'll get down to the trading."

There was only one ship left of the British Squadron. Its port and starboard lights glimmered prettily in the dark. I supposed the other ships were out blockading a river or chasing a Spanish slaver. They had not approached us.

"How is it the British haven't gone after the Captain on his trips ashore?" I wondered aloud.

"We've a perfect right to sell and trade our goods," said Purvis indignantly. Then he laughed. Once, he said, a real African king had come aboard—"Then they do have kings," I said broodingly. "Well, naturally, they have kings," exclaimed Purvis. He went on with his story, telling me the king and the Captain had got so drunk that when dawn rose, the Captain had clambered over the side, ready to make off and rule the tribe and leave the black king in command of the ship.

"Drink turns people round," commented Purvis somewhat importantly.

"It's not drink," I protested. "It's the kidnapping of these Africans that turns everyone round!" And I looked with growing fear toward that shore which lay behind the turbulent waves whose ghostly white crests were visible in the darkness. I thought of the pyre of the barracoon, empty beneath a moonless sky that now and then let drop a brief weak fall of rain. I thought of the African kings setting upon each other's tribes to capture the men and women—and children for all I knew—who would be bartered for spirits and tobacco and arms, who would, any night now, be dropped into the holds of this ship. And all at once, I saw clearly before me, like a shadow cast on a sail, the woman in the garden in New Orleans, Star, standing so quietly in the doorway. The world, I told myself, was as wicked a place as our parson had said, although he was a great fool. I turned to Purvis, wanting to tell him about the woman in the garden.

He was staring down at me as though I was a cockroach, his jaw hanging loose, his hand raised above my head in a way I could not mistake. I ducked.

"Don't say such things!" he bellowed. "You know nothing about it! Do you think it was easier for my own people who sailed to Boston sixty years ago from Ireland, locked up in a hold for the whole voyage where they might have died of sickness and suffocation? Do you know my father was haunted all his days by the memory of those who died before his eyes in that ship, and were flung into the sea? And you dare speak of my parents in the same breath with these niggers!"

"I know nothing about your father and mother," I said in a voice that trembled. "Besides, they were not sold on the block."

"The Irish were sold!" he cried. "Indeed, they were sold!"

"They are not sold now," I muttered. But he raved on, and I sank to the deck, covering my ears with my hands. How could he object to one thing and not another? It made no sense at all! But my speculations were cut short. Purvis delivered a kick on my shin. I howled. As though he were cursing me, he said, "Get those buckets in the hold. Hurry up about it, you nasty piece of business!"

"What buckets?" I asked, wiping my tears away, for he had really hurt me.

He grabbed me up off the deck, and pointed to a row of buckets lined up nearby.

"What for? Why? Where shall I put them?" I asked, sobbing.

"They're latrines for the blacks," he replied, thunder echoing in his voice the way it does in a heat storm. "Put them where your fancy strikes you. It won't matter to *them*."

We did not say one word to each other the next day, and when he had an order to give me, he had Claudius Sharkey pass it on. But the next night's event ended our quarrel as well as the drinking of the crew.

At midnight, or thereabouts, I heard a sound as though a thousand rats were scrambling up the hull of *The Moonlight*. I sprang from my hammock, found myself alone in our quarters, and raced up the ladder to the deck.

In the clear sky, a great white moon hung poised above the main-mast, striping the deck with pale unearthly rays. The crew stood silently, their pistols in their hands, their backs against the port rail. Spark and Captain Cawthorne were at attention near the starboard rail. The carronade had been moved and was pointing its muzzle at a spot not far from the two officers.

I heard the cold dead clang of metal striking wood.

I heard one piercing scream. My teeth began to chatter.

Then a very small brown face rose above the rail as though it had flown up from the sea. It continued to rise slowly until its brown bare chest was visible. Then I saw dark hands around its waist. The hands lifted, the little naked girl's legs flew out, and I saw the head of the young man who had been carrying her.

For a second, she sat on the deck, looking all around, her eyes huge with amazement, then she crawled and jumped toward the rail but was forced back by the forward propulsion of the man who tot-tered over the rail, unable, it seemed, to bring his body any further. The child hugged the young man's neck frantically and buried her face in his hair. At that moment, Nicholas Spark bent his thin length and gripped the man's back as though he were gathering up cloth, and yanked him altogether over, the chains around his ankles striking the deck with a violent clanging.

The clanging never ceased as one after another of the captives struggled over the rail and were dropped or dragged onto the deck. How long did it all take? I'll never know. None of us moved.

Later, after the thud of bodies and the rise and fall of the sobs of the children had stopped, a group of nearly naked individuals sat hunched up beneath the tarpaulin we had rigged up. The Captain was aft, speaking in low tones to the *cabociero* who, this time, was accom-panied by a tall black man carrying a whip. Spark stood close to the blacks, his pistol in his hand.

Although many were silent now, some continued to lament. I prayed they would stop for I had not drawn a true breath since the child's face had appeared at the railing, and I wondered, gasping, when I would again.

"Purvis!" cried Spark suddenly. "Get to that one!"

Spark's pistol pointed at a man who squatted by himself, somewhat apart from the others. His knees were tight against his chest; his head lolled in a strange way. Purvis ran to him, lifted him up, yanked him back and forth, punched his arms and threw him about so violently I was sure they would topple overboard.

The other blacks, except for the little girl who had been the first over the rail, turned away from the sight. But she ran crying toward the young man.

"Grab her, Stout!" called Spark. Stout stepped forward and took the child by her hair, shoving her back among the others. He came back to where we were standing, smiling vaguely and rubbing his hand against his shirt.

"Get a measure of rum, Jessie!" Purvis shouted to me.

I fetched it from the galley and ran to Purvis who by now had backed the young man up against the rail.

"Pour it in his mouth," Purvis said.

"His mouth is shut," I said in a whisper.

"Open it!"

"How?"

"Here," said Stout, suddenly appearing next to us. He took the cup from my hands, lifted it, then shoved it forcefully against the man's clenched lips, grinding it back and forth like a shovel teasing hard earth, until trickles of blood dripped down the brown skin and onto Stout's fingers. I was aware the other blacks had all grown silent. The only sound was the muttering of the Captain aft, and the crunch of cup against teeth until the spilling moonlight revealed rum and blood mixed upon the deck.

When, that night, I lay awake in my hammock, I saw again and again my arm reaching up to the young man's dazed face, the rum dripping over the rim of the cup because of the trembling of my hand. I heard, hardly muffled by the timbers which separated me from them, the blacks groaning and crying out in the hold, and the world I had once imagined to be so grand, so full of chance and delight, seemed no larger and no sweeter than this ship. Before my tightly closed eyelids floated the face of the child who had, after that one glance at us all, seemed to comprehend her whole fate.

I wished Purvis was nearby, but he was on extra duty above the hold. I heard Gardere snoring a few feet away from me. I could not bear the silence. I woke him. He grumbled threateningly and cursed me for a troublesome rat.

"Why was that man treated that way?" I asked, ignoring his complaints.

"What man?"

"The one who was forced to drink the rum?"

"Man?"

"That Purvis was flinging about so . . ."

"You mean the nigger!"

"Him," I said.

Gardere sighed and pointed at his sea chest. "Get me some tobacco and my pipe, will you, lad?"

I handed him the articles he'd asked for. He took a long time lighting up. Then, expelling a cloud of smoke, he said, "When they sit that way, their heads on their knees, not moving at all, you must get them on their feet and distracted, by flogging sometimes. They will die if left in that condition."

"But die! How?"

"I don't know how. I've seen it happen though, I swear! They have no poisons since they could not conceal them, being naked as they are. But, somehow, they die. Try holding your breath, you'll see the difficulty. I tried it myself once after the first time I saw it happen. It bothers me to this day. It's a mystery. They ain't like us, and that's the truth."

For four nights, the long canoes slid alongside *The Moonlight*, giving up their burdens of blacks, those from the bottom of the boats half-conscious from the press of the bodies of their fellow captives, some bleeding from the ankle shackles which, as a consequence of the way they had been forced to lie, had bruised and broken their flesh.

Each night the crew, after loading the canoes with rum and tobacco and a few rusty weapons, gathered on the deck. In silence, we watched the blacks drag themselves beneath the tarpaulin, at least those who were not kicked under it by Spark's boots. The *cabociero* observed the arrival of his merchandise with unconcealed self-importance. Next to him stood the tall black man with his whip whose expression seemed to me to be one of utter loathing for white and black alike, as though there was not a race of men he would claim as his own. Once only, Cawthorne shoved a man toward the *cabociero*.

"A macaroon!" cried Cawthorne. "You dishonest heart! To try and trick me with inferior goods after all the concessions I've made you!"

Purvis explained to me that a macaroon was a black too old for any use, or one with physical defects of some kind.

"What will happen to him?" I asked.

"It's none of our affair," growled Purvis, giving me a warning look. I had guessed by now that any interest, much less concern, I showed about the blacks meant to Purvis that I was demeaning his mother and father. It was as though there was a connection in his mind, unknown even to himself, between our living cargo and those Irish folk long dead, the story of their voyage a lingering and bitter glory in his memory.

Our holds were pits of misery. Two men were found dead the second morning, and Stout dumped their bodies over the side as I dumped waste. Curry cooked up messes of horse beans on deck. Many of the slaves spat them out. They were given yams, a store of which had been brought aboard by the *cabociero*. These seemed to suit them better. But the yams, I learned, were only doled out while we were still in sight of land. Once at sea, they were doomed to a diet consisting largely of the beans with an occasional piece of salt beef taken from our own stores. Along with their two daily meals, they received a half pint of water.

"More than we'll get," Purvis said. "When the supplies run low, it's us who'll go without. There's no loss to Cawthorne if we starve to death or die of thirst."

On our last morning, the little girl—the first to be brought aboard *The Moonlight*—was carried to the rail by Stout. He held her upside down, his fingers gripping one thin brown ankle. Her eyes were open, staring at nothing. Foam had dried about her mouth. With one gesture, Stout flung her into the water. I cried out. Ned smacked me across the face with such force I fell to the deck. When I got up, I saw a boy close to my own age, staring at me from among the group of silent slaves squatting beneath the tarpaulin. I could not read his expression. Perhaps he was only looking past me to the shore of the land from which he'd been taken.

The Captain had picked up a piece of news during one of his earlier sorties ashore. One of the two American cruisers known to be patrolling the African coast had been sighted from Cape Palmas off the Windward Coast. With nearly 100 slaves in our holds, the Captain was in a fever lest some word had been gotten to the Americans by the British. You would have thought the whole of the British Navy had only one purpose in mind—to prevent Cawthorne's pursuit of his "God-given trade."

It had grown fearfully hot, the sun blasting us with its rays from its first rising. Our water ration had been reduced again, and I went about my duties with a mouth as dry as ashes. I no longer searched the holds for rats. I had a new job—to empty the bucket latrines as they were handed up to me by Benjamin Stout who, moving across the recumbent bodies in the holds, went about his work as though stepping on cobblestones.

It was with relief, a strange feeling after these days, that I learned we were to set sail for São Tomé, a Portuguese-held island to the south where we would take on water and food.

After that, our direction would be toward the west, along the equator, then northwest as far as the Cape Verde Islands.

It was there, Claudius Sharkey told me, that we would make speed, for we could catch the northeast trade winds, and be in the waters of Cuba in three weeks—with luck, after a thousand miles where the doldrums might hold us captive for days.

My heart sank.

I had believed that half this journey was over. But now, it seemed, it was at its true beginning.

Nicholas
Spark Walks
on Water

. . . AND THEN, one by one, each slave and each member of the crew went blind," Purvis related, "and the Captain and the officers hid in their quarters for fear they would catch the horrible disease. But they ran short of food and water and were forced out. Then the First Mate went blind, and one by one, the officers lost their sight. Blind, they roamed the decks. Blind, they found no drink or food. The Captain determined to escape the ship in the small boat. But he was so desperate, he broke his arm trying to disengage the boat and lower it to the water. And so he was alone with the dead and the dying beneath the blazing sun. And the ship was loose upon the sea, flung here and there as the sea wished, and no one has seen it to this day."

"But how is it known that the Captain broke his arm?" I asked.

"Ah . . ." sighed Seth Smith, "we just know." The weak light from the oil lamp cast shadows shaped like spoons on the faces of the men. Gardere had shut his eyes tight as though blinded by Purvis' story.

"Other ships passed it by before it disappeared," Purvis said to me in that tone of absolute conviction I'd heard before in the men's voices when they'd told tales that were more invention than truth. "And a certain Captain swore he saw the small boat hanging at such an angle from its davits that it was clear the Master of that ship had made an unsuccessful attempt to lower it and harmed himself."

I could not follow Purvis' reasoning at all, yet there was a sense of truth about the story, at least about the horror of it.

"Is there no cure for such a disease?" I asked.

"None," replied Ned. "No more than there's a cure for man himself." I stared at him, still wondering why he'd given me such a blow when I'd cried out at the sight of the dead child. I hoped he'd been trying to protect me. I knew now how the crew responded to any sign of my distress at the plight of the blacks.

"Never mind that, Ned," said Gardere sulkily, opening his eyes wide. "You're not a saint, you know." Gardere's voice was thick as though his throat was full of honey, and his words were faintly slurred. All the men had been drinking heavily ever since Gardere and Purvis had come off watch. Even though it was so late, they had not, as was their habit, flung themselves instantly into their hammocks.

We had weighed anchor and sailed that evening so the slaves would not see the shore of their homeland disappearing, and a fresh land wind was bearing us along smoothly. But the men were not eased by our progress; their mood was restless and shadowed by gloom. All day, they'd been telling each other stories of lost ships although none so dreadful as the one I'd just heard.

But the stories did not drown out the sounds from the holds. Not all the gabble of the sailors, the sustained flow of the wind that drove us on, could mask the keening of the slaves as they twisted and turned on the water casks, or struggled to find an edge of one of a handful of straw pallets upon which to rest their shackled ankles. I dozed. I woke. Never to silence. Would it go on this way to the end of our voyage? Sharkey claimed they would settle down. Settle down to what?

It seemed that Benjamin Stout was to be in charge of the slaves. Next day, he raced from one task to another. Although I had grown to dislike the slowness of his walk and gesture, I found his energy even more repulsive. He saw to the water rations, to Curry's activities with the huge cauldron. Frequently, he hung over the holds, shouting down a few words of the African language. I asked Ned if he, too, could speak African. He told me there were as many languages in Africa as there were tribes but since none of them were Christian he would not corrupt his tongue by learning a single word from any of them. Did he know, I asked him, what people we carried on our ship? Ashantis, he'd replied with disgust, probably captured in tribal wars with the Yoruba.

"But the children don't battle, do they?" I asked.

"The chiefs kidnap the children," he replied. "The slavers give good trade goods for them because they fetch such high prices in the West Indies." He looked contemptuously toward the now distant shore, more like a low-lying cloud than land. "The African was tempted and then became depraved by a desire for the material things offered him by debased traders. It's all the Devil's work."

I looked at him curiously. "But you're a slaver, ain't you, Ned?"

"My heart's not in it," he said flatly. I wondered about his heart, imagining it to be something like one of the raisins Curry used to slip into the duff.

We hadn't had such a good thing to eat as duff in many weeks. Being on a ship and eating from its stores was like a man burning down his house to keep warm.

I had not yet been seriously afflicted with the thing called seasickness. But early the next morning, we hit a strange turbulence in the sea so that *The Moonlight* pitched forward, then rolled sideways in such rapid alternation that my stomach did likewise. I took only a swallow of water. I felt that if I didn't keep my mouth tightly closed, I should be turned inside out like a garment that was to be laundered.

If the ship's wild pitching made me ill, it drove the blacks below into frenzies of terror. Howls and cries rose out of the holds unceasingly. The ship herself seemed to protest the violence of the water, whining and creaking more loudly than I'd ever heard her.

Ben Stout, the Captain and Spark appeared untouched by the suffering of our cargo. I can't say the rest of the crew took pity on the miserable creatures in their dark places below the deck, but the men were silent, and avoided the holds as much as they could.

The Captain had had his chair lashed close to the wheel and did not leave it until we were free of this convulsion of the sea. Spark had joined Stout near the holds, wearing his pistol and carrying the same tarred rope with which Purvis had been flogged. Spark never looked down no matter what sounds issued from below. Then I forgot my sick stomach, forgot everything.

As he left his chair, the Captain shouted, "Tell Bollweevil to get his pipe." Gardere glanced briefly at me from his position at the helm. I could not read his expression.

With a small smile, Stout said, "Get ready to play your music, lad," then reached out his hand to pat my shoulder. I moved back quickly as though a cottonmouth had struck in my direction. I saw, as clearly as I could see the cat-o'-nine-tails in his other hand, those fleshy fingers gripped around the ankle of the dead little girl.

I went below and got my fife, but stood unmoving in the dark until I heard them shouting for me.

The slaves from one of the holds were being hoisted one by one to the deck. Only the women and the youngest children were unshackled.

In just a few days, they had become so battered, so bowed by the fears that must have tormented them, that they could barely stand up. They blinked in the bright white light of the growing day. Then they sank to the deck, the women clutching weakly at the children, their shoulders bent over as though to receive the blows of death.

All hands were present; even Ned was ordered to leave his work-bench and stand to attention.

The slaves were given their water rations and fed rice with a sauce of pepper and oil. When they saw the food and water, sighs rose from them like small puffs of wind, one following so close on the other that in the end, it seemed one great exhalation of air.

"Some of them think we eat them," whispered Purvis to me. "They think that first meal was only to fool them. When they see we intend to keep on feeding them, they grow quite cheerful."

I saw no cheer. The adults ate mournfully, the food dribbling from their lips as though their spirits were too low to keep their jaws firm. The children spoke among themselves. Sometimes a woman held a child's head as though she feared its voice might draw down punish-ment upon it, and rice from the child's mouth would spill across her arm.

When they had finished their meal, the Captain said to Stout, "Tell them to stand up. And tell them we have a musician for them and that they are to dance for me."

"I can't tell them all that, Sir," Stout replied. "I don't know their words for dancing or for music."

"Then tell them something to get them to their feet!" cried the Captain angrily as he flourished his pistol.

Stout began to speak to the slaves. They did not look at him. Some stared up at the tarpaulin as though there were a picture painted on it; others looked down at their feet.

We had formed a circle around them, dressed, shod, most of us armed. Many of them were naked; a few had ragged bits of cloth around their waists. I glanced at the sailors. Ned's eyes were turned upward toward heaven. I supposed he was reporting to God on the folly of everyone else but himself. But the rest were staring fixedly at the slaves. I felt fevered and agitated. I sensed, I saw, how beyond the advantage we had of weapons, their nakedness made them helpless. Even if we had not been armed, our clothes and boots alone would have given us power.

There was something else that held the attention of the men— and my own. It was the unguarded difference between the bodies of the men and women.

I had told no living soul that on some of my late walks through the old quarter at home, I had dared the chance of hell fire by glancing through the windows of certain houses where I had seen women undressing, and undressed. I can only say that I didn't *linger* at those windows. Sometimes, after my peeking, I had been ashamed. Other times, I had rolled on the ground with laughter. Why I was chagrined in one instance and hilarious in another, I don't know.

But what I felt now, now that I could gaze without restraint at the helpless and revealed forms of these slaves, was a mortification beyond any I had ever imagined.

At the increasingly harsh shouts of Ben Stout, some of the black men had risen, swaying, to their feet. Then others stood. But several remained squatting. Stout began to lay about him with the cat-o'- nine, slapping the deck, flicking its fangs toward the feet of those who had not responded to his cries with even a twitch. At last, he whipped them to their feet. The women had risen at the first word, clutching the small children to their breasts.

"Bollweevil!" called the Captain.

Ned suddenly lit up his pipe.

I blew. A broken squeak came out of my fife.

"Tie him to the topmost crosstrees!" screamed Cawthorne. Stout, smiling, started toward me. I blew again. This time I managed a thin note, then some semblance of a tune.

The cat-o'-nine slapped the deck. Spark clapped his hands without a trace of rhythm. The captain waived his arms about as though he'd been attacked by a horde of flies. A black man drooped toward the deck until Spark brought his heel down on his thin bare foot.

I played on against the wind, the movement of the ship and my own self-disgust, and finally the slaves began to lift their feet, the chains attached to the shackles around their ankles forming an iron dirge, below the trills of my tune. The women, being unshackled, moved more freely, but they continued to hold the children close. From no more than a barely audible moan or two, their voices began to gain strength until the song they were singing, or the words they were chanting, or the story they were telling overwhelmed the small sound of my playing.

All at once, as abrupt as the fall of an axe, it came to a stop. Ben Stout snatched the fife from my hands. The slaves grew silent. The dust they had raised slowly settled around them.

That morning, I danced three groups of slaves. In the last, I saw the boy who I thought had looked at me when I cried out at Stout's heaving the child overboard. He wouldn't stand up. Spark dealt him a mighty blow with the tarred rope which left its tooth on the boy's back, a red channel in the tight brown flesh. He stood then, moving his feet as though they didn't belong to him.

It was to perform this service every other morning that I had been kidnapped and carried across the ocean.

I dreaded the coming of daylight. I listened without interest to rumors—that two of the slaves had fever, that the ship we had seen to windward was an American cruiser in pursuit of *The Moonlight*, that Spark had suddenly taken to drink, that Stout was the Captain's spy among us, that a black child had the pox.

In the harbor of São Tomé, in the sickly haze of a morning when I'd been relieved of all my duties save that of emptying the latrine buckets, I wondered if I dared leap overboard and take my chances on reaching the shore. But what would I find there? Other men who might use me worse than I was being used? Or a captain who tortured his own crew? God knows, I had heard of such things!

Now the slaves were fighting among themselves. The immediate cause was the latrine buckets. Many of them could not reach them quickly enough across the bodies of the others, for there was not a spare inch of space. Most of them had what Purvis called the bloody flux, an agonizing affliction of their bowels that not only doubled them up with cramps but made the buckets entirely inadequate.

One night as we lay at anchor, waiting for the morning when fresh supplies would be loaded on the ship, I heard a scream of inhuman force, of intolerable misery. I began to weep helplessly myself, covering my mouth with an old cap of Stout's for fear one of the crew would hear me.

We sailed from the island shortly, with no regrets on my part. It was as though I was trying to swallow the long days ahead, to stuff them down my throat, to make them pass with a gulp, thinking of that hour, that minute, when I would be let off this ship.

When we were two days out on our westward course, I heard once again that cry from one of the holds, a woman's scream, hair-raising, heart-squeezing. I had been dancing a group of slaves, and at that terrible sound, Spark signaled me to stop my tune. Stout ran to the hold from which the cry had issued. He disappeared down it. Not a minute later, a black woman was tossed upon the deck like a doll of rags.

"Over!" said the Captain. Spark and Stout lifted the woman, who was alive, carried her to the rail and swung her up and over. We didn't hear the splash she must have made when she hit the water, but then we were making speed before a fair breeze.

"She had the fever," Stout said to me as he passed, "and was dying and would have infected the rest of them." He was not trying to excuse himself. No, it was only his usual trick. He knew I thought he was evil, but he liked to suggest that beneath that I held another opinion of him, that, in fact, I admired him. It was a complicated insult.

The slaves were all looking at the place where the woman had been thrown overboard. Sick and stooped, half-starved by now, and soiled from the rarely cleaned holds, they stared hopelessly at the empty horizon.

I found a dreadful thing in my mind.

I hated the slaves! I hated their shuffling, their howling, their very suffering! I hated the way they spat out their food upon the deck, the overflowing buckets, the emptying of which tried all my strength. I hated the foul stench that came from the holds no matter which way the wind blew, as though the ship itself were soaked with human excrement. I would have snatched the rope from Spark's hand and beaten them myself! Oh, God! I wished them all dead! Not to hear them! Not to smell them! Not to know of their existence!

I dropped my fife on the deck and fled to my hammock. I would stay there until I was forcibly removed.

Which I was, soon enough.

They sent Seth Smith to get me.

"Get down!"

"Damn you all!" I said.

"If I have to carry you, it'll go hard for you."

I gripped the edges of my hammock. He turned it over with one movement of his hand, then caught me round the waist and took me to the deck.

The slaves had been returned to the hold. Captain Cawthorne was holding my fife in his hand, turning it idly. Standing next to him was Ben Stout. The fife reflected bright bits of sunlight.

"We won't have none of that," the Captain remarked. I recalled Purvis' mad song to himself about some of this and some of that. Purvis was nowhere to be seen. Ned was bent over his bench, a piece of chain in his carpenter's vise. I only noticed now that he was extremely thin, and that he looked ill.

"You're not so young you don't know what an order is," the Captain said. He shoved the fife at my chest and poked about with it as though trying to discover what I had concealed beneath my shirt.

"Stand to the rail," he ordered.

I did. The sea was blue today.

"Five," said the Captain.

Five times, Stout brought the rope down on my back. I had been determined not to cry out. But I did. It hurt more than I could have imagined. But I was not ashamed of my cries, for each time the rope fell, I thought of the slaves, of the violent hatred I had felt for them that had so frightened me that I had defied Master and crew. My eyes flooded with tears. The taste of salt was in my mouth. But as the blows fell, I became myself again. That self had gone through such transformations, I could not claim to be altogether familiar with it. But one thing was clear. I was a thirteen-year-old male, not as tall though somewhat heavier than a boy close to my own age, now doubled up in the dark below, not a dozen yards from where I was being beaten.

Seth Smith did not look at me as he carried me back to my hammock. Through the red haze which at the moment afflicted my vision I saw a stupid determination in his face like that I had observed on the features of drunken men who fight at any excuse.

Later, Ned came to tend my back, and Purvis showed up, scratching himself and snorting and making every effort to appear at ease.

"Don't feel too bad, Jessie," he said. "There's not a sailor living who's not felt the lash."

"Don't tell him such nonsense," protested Ned. "Don't make out it's an honor to be beaten. It's all because of greed and its festering excuses."

They bickered back and forth but they spoke in whispers, perhaps to spare me their noise. I paid no attention for my emotions were changing from second to second, and I had no interest in anything else as my rage against Ben Stout gave way to hopelessness at the thought of the weeks ahead, and hopelessness in its turn was vanquished by the intense pain that spread out from my back until my very toes throbbed with it.

They left me to myself at last, but not before Purvis had offered me beer, saying it would cure me entirely—which it didn't. It was only then my brain steadied. I think it must have steadied, for I felt an extraordinary sad tranquility, that same sad and empty calm the sea had on certain cool mornings when you knew it would look the same if you weren't there to see it.

I knew Stout would come creeping about with some explanation, so that when he did, I was not surprised.

"I laid the rope lightly on you, Jessie," he said. "You know, don't you, I could have done much worse? Well—I can see that you're angry with me—and I would be the same if it had been you—"

"I don't want to hear you speak," I said as coldly as I could. "Not now, never again."

"I wouldn't be so impertinent if I was you, lad," he remarked softly. "I have the Captain's good will, and there's none else on this ship that has!"

"Who else *would* he fancy except you?" I replied. He could do me no worse than he had done, and right now I didn't care if he tossed me into the sea.

He sighed and shook his head, then smiled down at his own hand as though only he and it could comprehend my backwardness.

My wounds healed. But the ship and its crew, among whom I once imagined I had taken root, learning each man like a new language, and even developing some skill in small tasks about the ship, had become as remote from my understanding as were the lands that lay beneath the ocean. I became cautious. I observed the sailors with as little pity as they observed the blacks. As for them, I shuddered at the barbarousness of chance which had brought each of them to our holds, although, as I had good reason to know, chance often wore a suit of clothes, and sometimes chewed tobacco, and carried a pistol.

Except for Ned, who held all living men in low esteem. I saw the others regarded the slaves as less than animals, although having a greater value in gold. But except for Stout and Spark and the Captain, the men were not especially cruel save in their shared and unshakable conviction that the least of them was better than any black alive. Gardere and Purvis and Cooley even played with the small black children who now roamed the deck with relative freedom, the sailors allowing themselves to be chased about if the Captain and Spark were not watching, giving the children extra water from their own slim rations and fashioning rough toys of wood to amuse them.

As for Spark, I concluded he was entirely brainless and evil only in the way that certain plants are poisonous. The Captain was dangerous, driven to hateful actions by his passion for what he described as "business." But Stout was like no one else. He could not be shamed; he would not show anger. And I could not help watching him, though I itched with irritation, and wearied my brain devising plots to catch him out in the open.

To relieve my feelings, I spoke of them to Purvis.

He listened soberly for once, and said, "I suppose you're right, Jessie. He's a bad one. You know he was tormenting that female we dropped overboard, don't you? Did you know it was him that drove the poor creature mad?"

I was astonished to hear him use the word *poor*, and it confused my sense of what he was saying.

Seeing by my expression that I was baffled, although not guessing the cause, he exclaimed impatiently, "The nigger woman, the nigger woman!"

"But what did he do to her?" I asked.

"I didn't see it, but Isaac told me he had her up on deck during his watch. He was speaking to her in that language of theirs, and she was weeping and wailing, then Stout would strike her across the face, then speak some more until she fell on the deck in a fit. God knows what stories he was telling her! It's a curse for the blacks he speaks their tongue. You can be sure he addles their minds with his tales."

"But why didn't the Captain interfere?"

"The Captain! He cares nothing for what's done to them as long as they can still draw breath. And he doesn't know about Stout and the nigger woman. Why, I believe he'd have the dead ones stuffed if he thought he could sell them so! And when he loses a few, he still has the insurance. He can always say he jettisoned the sick ones to save the healthy. And he'll collect! He always has. And if they're all sickly when we get where we're going, there's many a trick for hiding their condition. Anyhow, the planters will buy them no matter what, for if they drop dead in the fields, there's an endless supply of them."

We hit a spell of bad weather. There were fitful winds, and days with no wind when the sea lay around us like a brazen platter. The fights among the crew were louder than those among the slaves. Our rations were minimal. The ship echoed with a noise such as crows make battling for tree space. Between the wet and wind of squalls, and the heat and haze of windless days, there was not a moment of ease.

My stomach rebelled. I was ill all the time. Barely able to stand, I danced the slaves, seeing how the men's ankles had been gnawed at by their shackles as though the metal things were vicious and alive. They could hardly move to my tunes. Often, only Stout and myself attended the grim ceremony in the morning. I hated what I did. I tried to comfort myself with the thought that, at least, it gave them time out of the hold. But what was the point of that or of anything else?

The Moonlight had long since lost her sleek look—the deck was filthy, the ship stank to the heavens, the men dressed themselves in what lay closest to hand, the drinking started again, and the drunken-ness spewed itself out in anger and bewilderment.

I remembered one of the seamen telling me one could get used to anything. There was a half truth in that—if you were on a ship and there was no way off it save to drown. But I found a kind of freedom in my mind. I found out how to be in another place. You simply imag-ined it. I recalled every object in our room on Pirate's Alley. Each day brought with it the memory of something else until I think I could have counted the floorboards, traced upon the air the cracks in the walls, counted the spools of thread in the basket by the window. Then I would step outside and see the houses across the way, the cobble-stones of the street, the faces of neighbors.

When I was thus occupied, winning liberty from the ship, I boiled with rage if someone spoke to me. I could no longer trust my tongue, but though I feared I might, all unknowing, snap at Cawthorne him-self, I could not relinquish my dream of home.

Then, one morning, it began to penetrate through my fog of recol-lection that the young black boy was paying me heed. Aware of his eyes, I tried to move out of their range. Next time, he seemed as he lifted his feet to be moving close to me. I saw that Stout's attention, for the moment, was directed toward Ned who was half lying across his bench. I can't think what impulse moved me, but I took the fife from my lips and whispered my name to the boy. Only that. *"Jessie!"* And as I whispered, I pointed at myself. I began to play at once. The boy's eyes never left my face that morning.

There were days when one might have thought all was peaceful, when the wind was steady, the sun shone warmly from a cloudless sky, when the small black children tumbled and ran about and even laughed among themselves, when the holds had been cleaned, and the slaves sat quietly beneath the tarpaulin while the seamen gazed pensively across the rolling fields of the sea. It was a piece of magic, and for an hour or two I forgot the heat and smell and pain and had no cause to trouble myself with pictures of home. It never lasted long, and was itself like a dream.

Before we began our turn toward Cape Verde, several events occurred which affected the rest of our voyage. The first was the death of Louis Gardere on one of those dead calm mornings that filled us all with despair.

He had been at the wheel, the Captain at his side. Suddenly Gardere's face seemed to move off its bones; one shoulder twisted and turned as though it were not part of him. Then he dropped to the deck, his body twitching. Ned, clearly sick himself by this time, examined Gardere. He died an hour later, clutching his chest with his powerful hands and mumbling words we could not make out.

Purvis spoke of it all night, reviewing each moment, telling Ned it could not have been a heart seizure but was undoubtedly some fever Gardere had caught from the blacks.

As though to confirm Purvis, six blacks died that night. Ned, held up by Sharkey and Isaac Porter, examined their bodies.

"Fever," he said through pale dry lips, and fainted dead away. He was taken below where after a few minutes, he regained consciousness. He watched us with unblinking eyes. I felt the fear of the men, and my own fear. It was like the smell of the ship—it ran into every crack and cranny of my mind.

The crew sobered up. The ship made headway for several days and the men grew more cheerful. But Ned became thinner as though his substance was leaking away through his hammock. He would drink water now and then, or hold a bit of a biscuit soaked in wine in his mouth.

"What do you have, Ned?" I asked him.

"A touch of death," he whispered. I spilled the cup I had been holding to his lips. A faint grin stretched his mouth.

"Haven't you heard of the wages of sin?" he asked in a quavering voice. "Did you think they were gold?"

The day we changed our course for the northwest, Nicholas Spark took leave of whatever senses he had.

That morning, he'd indulged in one of his savageries, bringing his heel down on the feet of a black man who'd spat out his food. Before my eyes could take it in, the man leaped at Spark and gripped his throat in such a way the Mate could not get at his pistol. If it had not been for the intervention of Stout, Spark would have been strangled.

The black man was flogged until he was unconscious. At the first stroke of the whip, I'd gone to the galley and found Curry picking worms out of a piece of crusted beef. I shuddered in the greasy dark as his parrot fingers plucked and squeezed at the horrible white things. When, no longer able to bear Curry's hunting, I returned to the deck, I saw the beaten man hanging against the ropes that bound him to the mast. The blood was leaking from his back in dark streams. Stout, the whip in his hand, was speaking to the Captain, and Purvis was at the helm.

I had started toward our quarters when I caught sight of Spark staggering from the stern, his pistol held straight out in his hand. He fired at the black man whose back burst into fragments of flesh. Cawthorne spun to face the Mate, his face red with fury.

I don't know whether Spark was still dazed from his near escape from strangulation, or whether he really meant to point his pistol at the Master of the ship. But the Master had no such doubts.

In not much more time than it takes to tell it, Nicholas Spark was bound with a rope and pushed to the rail and there dropped over. Just before he disappeared beneath the water, I swear he took three steps.

I ran to hide beneath Ned's hammock. In the silence, I listened to his labored breathing.

Finally, I spoke. "Ned," I whispered. "The Captain's had the Mate thrown overboard."

"I ain't surprised," said Ned.

Then Purvis joined us and told Ned the whole story. Ned said nothing, but I said I'd never seen a man so angry at another man as the Captain had been at Spark.

"I should say so!" exclaimed Purvis. "Why he dared to shoot that black!"

"But I thought it was because he pointed his pistol at Cawthorne," I said.

"Oh, not at all, lad," replied Purvis. "Old Cawthorne's been through mutinies before. He never lost a hair! But Cawthorne knew the black would recover—they can survive floggings that would kill a white man a hundred times over—and Spark killed him. Don't you see. *There went the profit!*"

I heard a strange sound in our seabound cave, a sound like wind rustling dead leaves. It was Ned, laughing.

The Spaniard

Have you ever watched a cockfight, Jessie? You'd never guess a fowl had so much life in it till you saw one with murder in its eye. It moves so fast you can only tell where the beak struck when the blood spurts! It's the finest sight in the world! I'd like to have my own fighting cocks someday. I've devised a plan to make the viewing better. There's always some who can't see the pit over the heads of the others, but here's how I would do it—"

"Cooley, leave off with your birds!" Sam Wick interrupted. "It's only savages who'd take pleasure in such a spectacle. We've outlawed it in Massachusetts. As for owning anything, you'll be fortunate if you end your days with something over your head to keep off the rain."

"They've outlawed everything in Massachusetts," retorted Cooley without much fire. The two sailors fell silent. Both stared at the horizon which appeared to rise and sink as the ship rolled. I looked at their eyes, so wide, so empty, like the sea itself in that moment when the last colors of sunset have faded and darkness begins. So had they witnessed—if it can be called that—the casting overboard of Ned Grime's body that morning, and later, when the holds had been emptied, the discovery of eight of the blacks dead, five men, one woman and two children who had followed Ned into the waves. There was no one to say what anyone died from now.

That Sam Wick was from Massachusetts, my mother's birthplace, held my attention only a second. They had all come from somewhere, after all. It made no difference to me. I didn't care if in New York or Rhode Island or Georgia, the crew had wives and children, or parents, or brothers and sisters. We were all locked into *The Moonlight* as the ship herself was locked into the sea. Everything was wrong.

The slaves were nearer to death than the crew, although what they ate was not much worse than what we ate, and none of us, except the Captain and Stout, who had now assumed the duties of Mate, was ever free from thirst except when it rained. But we could walk the deck. I wondered if, in this circumstance, that was not the difference between life and death. And although Ben Stout could and did increase our misery with his captious orders, there was a limit. There were courts of inquiry to which the Captain would have to answer for unusual cruelty toward his crew—if a sailor had the endurance to pursue justice. If any of us ever saw the shore again . . .

Our northwestward course was steady except during one violent downpour. Though we were out of the doldrums, Purvis never left off exclaiming at our luck in not having been becalmed for weeks. His voice was fevered; his eyes bulged as he tried to convince me—perhaps, only himself—that it would be clear sailing ahead, only a brief passage now until he collected his wages and his share of the profit from the sale of the slaves.

"I'll never ship on a slaver again," he would say, over and over again. "Never, Jessie! You see if I don't keep my word!"

I danced the slaves under Stout's watchful eyes. He always found time to observe me at my task. I was determined to show no emotion in front of him. I gazed blankly at the rigging as though I was alone with a thought. But in truth I was so agitated I could hardly make my fingers work on the fife. Despite my intention, I could not help but see the wretched shambling men and women whose shoulders sank and rose in exhausted imitation of movement. They were all sick. I could count the ribs of the boy to whom I had once whispered my name.

It had been some time since the little children had played on the deck. I think they were too weak to crawl or run about. God knows how the slaves slept. I wondered if they hastened toward sleep as I did, for it was only then the hours passed without reckoning.

Once, on a night when Sharkey was making a commotion because of cramps in his belly, I went on deck and looked down into the forehold. I thought they'd all died. I heard not a sound. *The Moonlight* herself was bathed in moonlight. Sam Wick, on watch, passed me without a word. A small pool of yellow light shone near the Captain's quarters. I supposed he and Stout were in there, drinking brandy and eating decent grub. The dark water was streaked with the pale light of the moon. I thought that now I understood the phrase, "lost at sea."

I had, until that moment, been racing ahead of the ship to the door of our room, to the welcoming cries of my mother and Betty, when all this would lie behind me as unsubstantial as the moonlight. But now I felt no such certainty. A great timidity possessed my thoughts. There was nothing sure on earth except the rising and setting of the sun—and, when the sky was quilted over with black storm clouds and there was no line between earth and heaven, who could tell what the sun was doing?

Did the black people have any idea of what was ahead for them? If the ship made Cuban waters—if we were not overtaken by French pirates out of Martinique—if we escaped the British patrol and the United States cruisers—if they survived fever and flux and starvation and thirst?

"Stay away from the holds, lad," said the poisonous sweet voice of Ben Stout. "It disturbs them to be watched. You can understand that, can't you?"

As though he cared for what disturbed them! I slunk away toward our quarters, hoping Sharkey had quieted down by now, that Purvis had found something in Ned's old medicine case that had eased him. But I did not get far.

"Wait!" Stout commanded in his official voice. I stood, my back to him.

"I'd like a word with you," he said, wheedling now. I turned slowly. "I'm concerned about the crew," he said. "I want them in good spirits. We're well out of the Gulf of Guinea. It won't be long till we reach the trades. There's reason for good cheer."

"Not for some of us," I replied.

"There's always loss," said Stout. "It's taken into account by any sensible officer. But you'll be fine, Jessie. You're young and strong."

"So was Gardere. So were all the black people who died."

"Gardere!" he exclaimed and laughed loudly. "Gardere had eaten himself out with rum before you was born. As for the niggers, lad, they're actually better off drowned, if you think about it. Nothing more to worry them. You *could* look at it that way."

"I'll look at it the way I choose."

"I like your honesty," he said softly. "There's no one else I'd trust on this ship. That's why I asked you about the crew's spirits."

But he hadn't asked me.

"You want me to spy for you?" I asked. Ben Stout looked forgivingly up at heaven. What was he up to? Did he want to discover what Curry mixed with the cabbage to make it taste like swamp grass? Would he like to know that Cooley's ambition concerned fighting cocks? Or that Isaac Porter bit his nails like a man playing a mouth organ? Or that Purvis snored and mumbled in his sleep?

Or did he want to know what I thought of him? Was I to spy on myself?

"Take you," he said. "How are your spirits?"

"I can't answer that," I said.

"But you must know how you feel!" he exclaimed, a touch of heat in his voice. I was surprised.

"I feel this way and that way," I said, "but never the way I once did when I lived at home in New Orleans."

"I want a plain answer."

"*I hate this ship!*" I said with all the force I could with what little courage I had in the face of Stout's menace.

"Ah!" he sighed. A second later, I saw his teeth gleam. "That must mean you hate me too."

"I didn't say so," I said.

"Hatred poisons the soul," he observed. "It is an incurable ailment."

"I would like to go below."

"I've been so good to you," he continued. "I don't understand your ingratitude. They've all talked against me. I suppose that accounts for it."

I would say nothing further to him. He stood silently looking at me. I grew uneasy. Something weakened in me. There was a quality about his stillness, his silence, that was like a huge weight pressing against me. I took one step away. He held out his hand toward me. I remembered the slave woman he'd tormented, and I scrambled down the ladder. Sharkey was hunched over himself, rubbing his belly. Purvis shot a glance at me.

"You're as white as salt, Jessie! What is it?"

"I wish Stout was dead!" I cried.

"But he is dead," said Purvis. "He's been dead for years. And there's one of him on every ship that sails! There's someone makes little dolls of him and sprinkles them with gunpowder and steals along the docks and places a doll in each ship—and when it's out at sea, the doll grows and grows till it looks just like a sailor man, and it takes its place among the crew and no one's the wiser until two weeks at sea when one of the crew says to another, 'Ain't he dead? That one over there by the helm?' and the other says, 'Just what I was thinking— we've got a dead man on the ship—'"

Sharkey gave out a dog's yelp of laughter and at that, Purvis grinned broadly.

Whenever I saw a sail on the horizon—which was not often—I would pretend it was a British cruiser not afraid to displease the United States Government by boarding us. I imagined the slaves set free, the rest of us taken to England where Stout would be hanged, and Purvis and I sent by fast ship to Boston. From there, I would make my way home, and one day, in the freshness of a morning, I would open the door and step inside, and my mother would look up from her work, and—

But we were not pursued. And if we had been, it is unlikely *The Moonlight*, with all her sails stretched, could have been captured. Only pirates might take us, French pirates undeterred by any flag, eager to pounce on a tattered dirty little ship with a cargo of half-dead blacks, and a bunch of ailing seamen as hard and dry and moldy as the ship's biscuits they gnawed on.

When, one morning, I could not find my fife, I thought Cooley or Wick, longing for distraction, had hidden it from me. They swore they had not touched it. And no one else had either, said Purvis, be-cause he would have heard anyone sneaking about and reaching into my hammock where I always kept it. But Purvis had been on watch the night before.

I searched frantically throughout the ship. Porter came looking for me and told me I was wanted on deck. I found Stout waiting aft, the Captain standing a few feet away looking through his spyglass at the horizon. There had not been a word between Stout and me since the night I'd run away from him.

"We're going to bring up the niggers, Jessie," he said. "Where's your music maker?"

The instant he spoke, I knew Stout had made off with the fife.

I was dumb with fear; it rushed through me like heat from a fire.

"He's not got his pipe, Captain," Stout said gravely.

Cawthorne turned to look at me.

"What now?" he asked impatiently.

"I say, the boy is refusing to play—"

"I'm not!" I cried to Cawthorne. "It was beside me in my ham-mock last night! It's been taken from me!"

"Taken?" repeated the Captain. He scowled. "What are you both-ering me with such foolishness for, Stout? And what is this creature howling about? Take care of it yourself, man!" With that, he went to his spyglass.

"Come along," Stout said to me. "We'll look for it together."

I caught sight of Purvis watching us from across the deck. He'd been mixing up a batch of vinegar and salt water with which we sometimes cleaned out the holds. But he'd stopped his work to keep an eye on me. Without even looking in his direction, Stout called out, "Get on with it, Purvis!"

"I've already looked everywhere," I mumbled without hope.

"I can't hear you, lad," said Stout.

"I've looked everywhere!" I shouted.

"Well . . . I think it's in one of the holds," he said. "Yes. That's what I think. Someone has taken it and dropped it down to the niggers so they can play their own tunes." As he spoke, his thick fingers circled my throat. He pushed me to the forehold.

"You go down there and fetch it up," he said softly. "You're sure to find it there. Purvis likes such tricks, you know. It would be just like Purvis, wouldn't it? To have dropped it down there? Say you agree with me!"

He gave me a mighty shove and I fell to the deck.

"Hurry, Jessie! It's no good, your resting like that!"

I clung to the hatch coaming. Stout bent down and loosened my fingers. "Just drop down," he whispered. "They won't hurt you, lad." He swung me to my feet and pushed me so far I could not but look down. A patch of daylight washed across the twisted limbs of the slaves. I saw nothing that was not flesh.

"Hurry, now!" said Stout. Suddenly, Purvis was at his side.

"I'll look for it," he said.

"No. No you won't. He must take care of his responsibilities, Purvis. And what do you mean, neglecting your own, and listening in on what doesn't concern you?"

The hope that Purvis would save me had made me go slack. Then Stout lifted me up in the air the way a heron grips a fish, and suspended me over the hold.

"Oh, Lord! Don't drop me!" I screamed.

"You'll climb down as I want you to," he said. "And you'll look here and there until you find your pipe. After that, we can get on with things." As he spoke, he slowly brought me back to the deck. I caught sight of a blank face turned up toward the light. The man blinked his eyes, but there was no surprise written on his face. He had only looked up to see what was to befall him next. I went down the rope knowing my boots would strike living bodies. There was not an inch of space for them to move to.

I sank down among them as though I had been dropped into the sea. I heard groans, the shifting of shackles, the damp sliding whisper of sweating arms and legs as the slaves tried desperately to curl themselves even tighter. I did not know my eyes were shut until fingers brushed my cheeks. I saw a man's face not a foot from my own. I saw every line, every ridge, a small scar next to one eyebrow, the inflamed lids of his eyes. He was trying to force his knees closer to his chin, to gather himself up like a ball on top of the cask upon which he lived. I saw how ash-colored his knees were, how his swollen calves narrowed nearly to bone down where the shackles had cut his ankles, how the metal had cut red trails into his flesh.

All around me, bodies shifted in exhausted movement. I was a stone cast into a stream, making circles that widened all the way to the limits of the space that contained nearly forty people.

Suddenly I felt myself dropping, and I heard the wooden thunk of the two casks which I had, somehow, been straddling. Now I was wedged between them, my chin pressed against my chest. I could barely draw breath, and what breath I drew was horrible, like a solid substance, like suet, that did not free my lungs but drowned them in the taste of rancid rot. I tried to bend back my head, and I caught a blurred glimpse of Stout's face in the white sunlight above. With what I was sure was the last effort of my life, I heaved up the upper part of my body, but my legs had no leverage. I sank down. I began to choke.

Then arms took hold of me, lifting and pushing until I was sitting on a cask. I couldn't tell who'd helped me. There were too many entangled bodies, too many faces upon which not even an acknowledgment of my presence was written. I peered into the dark.

"You'll find it, boy!" Stout's voice floated down.

I sat without moving. To search the hold meant that I would have to walk upon the blacks. My eyes were growing accustomed to the shadowed corners not reached by the light from above. But my brain slept, my will died. I could do nothing. I felt a soft surge of nausea. I clapped my hand over my mouth as I tried to keep in whatever it was that so violently wanted to come out. Then, through my wet eyes, I made out a figure rising from the throng. It sank, then rose again. In its hand, it held aloft my fife. In the steaming murk, I recognized the boy. He pointed the fife at me. Another hand took hold of it, then another, until a third passed it to the man on the cask who managed to free one hand, take the fife and drop it on me. Someone groaned; someone sighed. I looked up to Stout.

"I was sure you'd find it, Jessie," he said.

I stood on the cask and flung out the fife. Stout reached down and took hold of my shoulders and dragged me up until I lay upon the deck.

"Now that you've found your instrument, we'll get on with the dancing," he said. "They must have their exercise."

I danced the slaves, aware that the shrill broken notes which issued from my pipe were no more music than were the movements of the slaves dancing.

Later, too weak and miserable to climb into my hammock, I sat on Purvis' sea chest, my head cradled in my arms. I heard the men moving around me but I did not look up. When someone touched me, I cried out.

"It's me, Jessie, it's me!" said Purvis.

I raised my head.

"Look here," he said.

Every finger of his hands was stretched. String was looped around each finger and it formed a design in the space between his hands. I think, for a second, I did not know where I was, remembering Betty holding out a cat's cradle to me in the candlelight. It was me who had taught her to take the strings from my hands, so forming a new cradle. Together, we'd invented a few, then I'd grown too old for such games. She would sit sadly by herself, the string ready to be transformed, waiting, until my mother, setting aside her work with a sigh, would go and turn the cradle inside out and Betty would smile.

"Take your thumbs and the first finger of each hand, see, and pinch these strings," Purvis said, wriggling his thumbs, "and pull them up and over. You'll see something startling!"

I stared up at him dumbly.

"Jessie! Do so I say!"

I took the string on my fingers. He rubbed his hands together and grinned, then delicately took hold of the string and brought it back to his own fingers.

"I see you know how," he said. "Again."

So we played cat's cradle until I lost one end off my little finger and the cradle snarled.

"I've brought you tea," he said. "Although it's cold as rain, drink it anyhow. It'll be sweet to your throat."

I drank it down.

"Listen, Jessie. We've hit the northeast trades now. It won't be long . . . three weeks, maybe. I wouldn't lie to you, would I? Only three weeks."

"I'm afraid of him," I said. I found no comfort in Purvis' news. The worst was always about to happen on *The Moonlight*. What would it matter if it was only three days? Misery hasn't got to do with clocks.

"I won't let him beat you," Purvis said fiercely.

"It's the other things he can do," I muttered.

"Sharkey's warned him," Purvis whispered. I thought it a measure of Stout's power to dismay that though he wasn't around, the very idea of him subdued Purvis, made him whisper, made him glance over his shoulder uneasily. "Sharkey's told him what we'll do to him when we get ashore. He's told him we'll track him down to wherever he goes if he harms you."

I felt a deep thrust of fear, although I couldn't tell if it was for Sharkey or myself.

"I saw you flinch," Purvis said. "You mustn't let *him* see that! He sups on the fear he rouses up. Don't give him that! Go about your tasks. I'll see to it myself you get home. My word on that. You'll have land beneath your feet, Jessie, and no one to stop you from what you want to do. You go up on deck now and get the fresh air and make yourself strong again."

He swayed a little with the movement of the ship. I saw how thin he had grown, how his trousers hung shapelessly on him like that blanket Ned Grime used to keep about his shoulders. He scowled with concentration as he wrapped the bit of string around his fingers, then slid it off so it was like a little spool.

"You're a tidy man," I said suddenly.

"I am that," he replied.

I often recalled how Purvis had wrapped that string around his finger. It calmed my spirit and made me smile. It was comic, I told myself, to be so careful with a few inches of string on a voyage like this one.

Claudius Sharkey did not truly recover from his cramps. He bore the pained expectant expression of a man preoccupied with a sickness which he suspects will finish him off. It meant more work for the rest of the crew. Sharkey faltered on the rigging, cursing himself as he went aloft so slowly that he drew Stout's harsh attentions. But Sharkey bore jeers and threats with eerie patience.

"Is it always like this?" I asked Purvis.

"Worse," he said. "I sailed on a ship with 500 slaves in the hold and 30 crew. At the end, there was 183 slaves alive and 11 crew. The boatswain killed the cook with his own carving knife a foot from a water cask. The rest died of disease. The Captain took his bible and left that ship—and the sea. I've heard tales that he's a walking preacher now, goes to towns and villages and gets up on a box and tells people the world is going to end any day, and if there ain't no people, he tells the trees and the stones."

We ran steadily through the days. I remembered as if it was another life the first weeks I had spent on *The Moonlight*, how sunlight and waves and wind had held me fast during my waking hours in a kind of spell, how I had felt that I, too, was dashing forward, feeling the strength of my own body as though I'd never known before what it meant to rise in the morning like an arrow shot from a bow. But not now. There was only labor and thirst. Sometimes I leaned against Ned's bench and wondered why that old man had let his life run out into the sea, when he might as well have done his work on land and had a little house for his trouble, with a church nearby where he could've gone and comforted himself. There must have been something mad in him. It seemed to me that men who went to sea were all mad, pitting themselves against such hazards to win out against dying when death would take them anyhow.

From that bench one afternoon, I caught sight of a strange stirring in an otherwise calm sea. Running to the rail, I saw, turning slowly on their backs, hundreds of great white maggots with crescent mouths upon which were stitched horrible teeth. "Sharks," said Cooley. "Snap us up like flies."

And the next morning, I came on deck to find the ship, its sails furled, at rest on a gently rolling sea. Off the starboard side, gleaming in the sunlight as though each grain of sand on its shore held its own tiny sun, was a small island. Above, seagulls circled our naked masts ceaselessly uttering their begging cries. I looked at the empty shingle, counted six stunted palm trees and measured my height against a low bluff rimmed with sea grass.

"You'd like to get off there, wouldn't you, Jessie?" asked Purvis. "You wouldn't be happy for long. There's nothing to eat or drink. It's just a bit of land only fit for birds and crabs."

"Does it have a name?"

"Whatever name you want to give it . . . there's bits of land like that all over this world. They don't belong to no one. I don't care for the look of them myself. It's not right they should be so empty."

For the first time in many weeks, I wondered if I might truly reach home. Then, as I strained to get a closer look at the island, a thing flew up out of the water, a fish with all the colors of the rainbow playing among its scales. I gasped and pointed as another sprang from the sea, then another . . .

"Flying fish," said Purvis. "There's peculiar creatures in these waters."

"My mother has a sewing box," I said, "and just such a fish is carved on it, but I thought it was an imaginary thing."

"I've heard the Indians eat them," said Purvis. "I wouldn't want to eat anything that hadn't made up its mind whether it belonged in water or air."

"I don't wish to disturb your rest," a familiar voice broke in. "But there's work to be done."

Ben Stout was standing behind us holding an iron file. Purvis looked at him as thought he were a piece of decking. Then he said to me with an air of great confidence, "We'll be in Cuban waters in a day or so, and not long after that, we'll be on land again where men is the same height." And he shot a ferocious glance at Stout who took notice of it with a wistful smile.

"That's a worthy thought," Stout said, "and I'll think hard on it. Meanwhile, take this file." He held it out to Purvis who snatched the tool from his hand and left.

"You won't be dancing the slaves in a regular way no more, Jessie," Stout said to me. "But that don't mean you can take your ease."

I wanted to cry, *Get on with it!* But didn't dare. I ground my teeth instead.

"The buckets!" he shouted suddenly. I jumped. "The buckets!" he repeated. "I thought your heart bled for the niggers! See how you neglect them, lad!" He grabbed my arm before I could get away. "I haven't told you which hold, have I?" he asked gently. "You do have a bad temper, don't you, Jessie?"

I wondered if he would break my arm. All at once, he let go. "Go help Cooley in the forehold," he said without even looking at me.

When I reached the hold, I found two buckets waiting for me. I emptied them over the side, and went back to get more. Cooley was just hoisting a third bucket onto the deck. It was filled with dead rats. I guessed the slaves had killed them by breaking the beasts' necks with their shackles. I emptied the rats over too.

Later, when I had a moment to myself, I went back and stared at the island again. The shadows from the sea grass had lengthened and the sand had lost its morning glitter. The tiny bit of land looked cold and lonely. I went to where Purvis was kneeling in front of a black man. He was working away at the shackles with the file Stout had given him. There was blood on it. Behind the man stood a dozen or so others waiting their turns.

By midafternoon all the slaves were free of their shackles. They were on deck, most of them staring at the island which the ship's bowsprit wavered toward like a compass needle. I watched Isaac Porter scouring the shackles. Sharkey, who was standing next to me, shook his head.

"Cawthorne's a fool to hang on to those things," he said. "He knows better—he knows a slaver ain't just a ship carrying slaves. If we're caught with some of what we've got on this ship, we might just as well be caught with the slaves themselves. I know of masters who've burned their ships once they've unshipped their cargo—just to make sure there was no trace left of what they'd been doing. But Cawthorne's so greedy—he's like a man choking on one chicken bone while he's grabbing for another."

I looked at the black people standing silently on the deck. "Thirty must have died," I said. "Maybe more."

"It's a great day for them," Sharkey said, "now we've taken off their restraints."

"They could kill us . . ."

"Oh, no! It's too late for that. They'd not have been turned loose if there was any such danger."

"I wonder where they think they are," I muttered.

"They don't think much," responded Sharkey. "You can be sure they're glad to be alive! Ain't we all glad?" he asked, and clapped me on the back.

The hatches were left open. The slaves moved about the deck as freely as their physical distress permitted. I thought it strange that they touched nothing. The very youngest had such swollen bellies that if you'd not seen their hollow eyes, their legs as thin and wrinkled as the limbs of old people, you might have thought them overfed. They showed no surprise at this new turn of events. They were beyond surprise. When they spoke, they kept their heads close together and their lips barely moved. At night, they went below to sleep. During the day we cleaned out the holds as thoroughly as we could while Stout bellowed down at us from the deck pretending we were not working as hard as we should.

"It's an utter waste of time," Purvis complained. "You can't ever get the stench out."

Three days after leaving the island, the Spanish flag flew from *The Moonlight*, giving us, declared Purvis, the right to anchor in Cuban waters off a serene stretch of coast that showed no sign of human habitation. "We're a Spanish ship now," he said, "and no American warship will take the chance of searching us and risk getting into trouble with the Spanish government."

"But if we're seen by a British warship?"

"Then we'll run up the American flag." His tone made it sound so easy, but his expression was grim.

"We're in danger from now on, aren't we?" I asked.

Purvis hesitated a moment, then said, "We've never been out of it. But it's worse when we unship the cargo."

We began to wait—as we had off the coast of Africa. There were lookouts posted day and night. On the second evening, I saw a light flicker from the beach. At the Captain's command, Sam Wick signaled back with a lantern and, like an idling star, the light flickered once again.

At midnight a boat drew alongside us. The night was warm and damp, and I'd come up to sleep on deck hoping that Cawthorne and Stout were sufficiently preoccupied with the approaching sale of the slaves not to bother about me and where I chose to berth. By lantern light, I observed the Captain standing by the rail grinning hugely into the dark as though to persuade it to smile back at him. A minute later, a tall black-haired individual sprang upon the deck accompanied by a black man who kept his head bowed as though it had grown that way. The tall individual was wearing a shirt so frilled and lacy that his chin appeared to be drowning in sea foam. The Captain bowed to him as if he were a lord. He did not return the bow, only looked about him with disgust. The two of them went to the Captain's quarters in front of which the black man stood like a sentinel.

"He's got no tongue," said Purvis who'd come to sit beside me. My scalp crawled. "Who's got no tongue?" I asked.

"The Spaniard's slave," replied Purvis. "I forgot why they cut it out of him. I think it even gave Cawthorne quite a turn when he found out about it. He don't like the Spaniard. Last time he drank up all the Captain's best brandy while they were haggling over money."

I said nothing. I had grown suddenly dizzy. I had had such fits before—seconds, sometimes whole minutes, when I did not know where I was, when everything grew strange and soft and blurred. I stared desperately at Purvis. Now that Sam Wick had moved away with the lantern, I couldn't see Purvis' eyes, but how immense his jaw was! His lips were moving. I heard nothing.

"Purvis!" I croaked.

He put his hand on my shoulder. I felt steadier.

"Haggling over money," he said again. That haggling had begun off the coast of Africa—now it was coming to an end here.

"That Spaniard is said to be the richest broker in Cuba," Purvis was saying. My ears sharpened. I felt the deck beneath me once again. "He bribes the highest officials," Purvis added admiringly.

"Why must he bribe them?"

"Why, the Spanish government is said to have undertaken to suppress the trade . . . of course they don't, no more than we do!"

"So all the governments are against the trade," I said, "and in the same way."

"I don't know about the Portuguese," Purvis replied in a thoughtful way.

"And do the British carry slaves in the holds of their anti-slavery warships?"

"No, not them!" said Purvis scornfully.

"How does the Spaniard get the slaves to the market?"

"They'll be taken off our ship in skiffs, and they'll be marched to a plantation a few miles inland. I went with Cawthorne last time. What grub we had! The plantation owner takes one or two of the best of the slaves, pays off the local magistrates all the way to Havana. That's where most of them will be sold."

"And when does Cawthorne get his money?"

"When the cargo has been unloaded," Purvis said.

I swallowed noisily. I could feel him peering at me in the dark.

"It's this last moment that's always the worst," he said, to comfort me I knew.

"Purvis? Where do you live?" I asked.

"Live? What do you mean?"

"Where's your home? Do you have a family?"

"A sister, older than me. That's all. She lives in Boston, or used to. I haven't seen her in fifteen years. She's dead for all I know." He was silent a moment. Then he said, "My home is where I'm at."

I thought of my home. If I ever got back, I would not, I told myself silently, ever go to the slave market on St. Louis and Chartres Streets again.

Ben Stout's
Mistake

For some time after the sun had set, the sky remained the color of rope. The ship lay steady on the glass-like surface of the water which was pricked, now and then, into small ripples when a seabird struck its surface. There was a smoky indistinct look to the Cuban shore. The birds disappeared, their last cries lingering in my ears the way strands of light cling briefly to the masts after the sun has vanished.

In the holds of the ship, in the crew's quarters, along hatchways, across the deck below the furled sails, there was constant and agitated movement on this last night the slaves would be aboard. Tomorrow, before dawn, they would be loaded into boats and taken away. Some, too weak to stand, would be lowered with ropes over the side of *The Moonlight* and, if they weren't too far gone, the Spaniard would see to it that they were strengthened and fattened for market.

A few lanterns were strung up to give us light. They made a mystery of the ship—we floated like a live ember in a great bowl of darkness.

"I don't like this weather," Purvis remarked. "I don't like Cuba. The sea is queer hereabouts."

If I had not felt so heavy-limbed and sleepy, I would have shouted with rage when Isaac Porter, resenting the fact he'd been ordered to go aloft and serve as lookout, gave me a hard blow across my back. But all I did was slump against the pile of tarpaulin Purvis and I had just taken down.

"It's a terrible life," Claudius Sharkey observed to no one in particular. As though he'd been summoned by Sharkey's words, Stout appeared suddenly. "Go to the Captain's quarters, Jessie," he said. "There's a chest there you are to bring out on deck."

I had not ever seen the inside of Cawthorne's roosting place and I was both curious and fearful. I went aft, half suspecting the errand was some trick of Stout's to get me into trouble. After entering a short passageway, I came to a heavy, elaborately carved door.

I knocked. A loud grunt left me perplexed as to what to do. "Well!" shouted the Captain's voice from behind the door. I went in. I was in a room, a real room, twice as spacious as the crew's quarters. I saw a large green chest near a berth covered with a scarlet rug. I had an impression of leather and new cloth, and I thought I smelled lemons.

"Well, Bollweevil," said the Captain with unusual mildness. He was sitting at a desk, his hands folded across a blood-red book, a lamp near his elbow.

"Stout sent me to fetch a chest, Sir," I said.

"That one," he said, waving one hand with its turnip-like fingers toward the green chest. I hesitated. "Take it," he said pleasantly enough. I grabbed hold of a ring in the side of the chest and pulled. Cawthorne held up his hands.

"Do you know what's inside?" he asked.

"No, Sir," I answered.

"Guess, then," he said.

I let go of the ring and straightened up. I felt a vague uneasiness as though someone I did not know was watching me from the shadows where the lamplight didn't reach.

"Well—"

"I insist," said the Captain, his voice hardening ever so slightly. "Rum?"

He laughed. "That's reasonable but incorrect," he said.

"Brandy?"

"Not at all! For those louts out there? Brandy?"

He rose to his feet and leaned toward me. "Guess again," he urged.

"Sir, I don't know!" I said pleadingly. I had had an impulse to ask him if he'd managed to pack a few more slaves in the chest. I was as afraid of what would pop out of my mouth as I was of him.

"Clothes," he said. "The very best! Silks, laces . . . for a little entertainment on our last night together. *They* like to dress up, and it amuses the men who are tired and discouraged now but who will cheer up soon enough."

Was I to take the chest? Or to listen? Before I could make up my mind, the Captain had reached somewhere behind his chair. "Here," he said, and held out a hand filled with biscuits. "If you'd guessed right, I wouldn't have given you a thing. Draw a moral from that—if you dare!"

I took the biscuits instantly, fearing he might change his mind, and stuffed them in my shirt.

"Thank you, Sir," I said.

Cawthorne scowled.

"You were sent to fetch the chest—then, fetch it!" he said, and sat down again and without another word opened the book and began to read it—or pretend he was reading it.

I lugged the chest out to the deck. Someone had set a keg of rum on Ned's bench. Because there was no wind to twist the flames, the lanterns burned steadily. Various crew members were lumbering about the deck in a way that reminded me of Bourbon Street. I looked around for Ben Stout and saw him standing a few feet away staring at the chest. He walked over to it, touched it, then told me to get my fife so I'd be ready.

"Ready for what?" I asked.

"For the festivity," said Stout, grinning.

When I returned to the deck with my fife, Stout had gone somewhere else. Sharkey and Purvis were talking together, leaning on the starboard rail and looking off into the dark the way we all often did. Most of the slaves were huddled near the bow of the ship; a few sat near the forehold, legs drawn up, shoulders bent, their faces hidden by their arms. Some of the women held sleeping children.

I heard the slap of oars. Soon, the Spaniard, his narrow fox head resting stiffly among his ruffles, made his appearance on board. With him was his servant who was wearing a striped jacket and a flat hat with a broad brim that hid his forehead. Cawthorne walked quickly to the Spaniard who pointed up at the Spanish flag. "A miracle!" he cried, then broke into a shriek of laughter. I did not see the joke of it although I did think the Captain's hat was comical. It was covered with gold scroll and was too large for him. I wondered if he had worn it for humorous effect, or whether, on the contrary, it showed how seriously he took himself. He was laughing along with the Spaniard. I saw him reach up to slap the tall man's back. The Spaniard shut his mouth at once and looked exceedingly put out. At the same time, the servant advanced a step closer to his master as though to protect him against Cawthorne's familiarity. Cawthorne's hand went to the pistol he carried. Then we were all distracted by Stout's shouting as he herded the slaves amidship. It was a sight that was both heartrending and ludicrous, for the black people were not resisting. They drifted toward the cluster of lanterns like shadow presences. Behind them, Stout, in a frenzy of self-importance, jumped up and down and waived his arms and commanded them to do what they were already doing.

Except for Porter far above us, we were all standing quite close together now, cargo, crew, Master, Cuban broker and his servant. For a moment, there was the whole heavy silence of the night, the sea. Then the Captain cried, "Open the chest!"

It was Stout who flung back the lid. Purvis muttered to me, "I didn't think he'd to it again—after the last time." "What?" I asked as I saw Stout tossing all kinds of garments on the deck, women's gowns, seamen's trousers, hats and capes and shawls and even lengths of cloth. "Give what he calls a ball," replied Purvis. "He says the niggers like to dress up and they ought to have a bit of pleasure before the Cubans get them. The Spanish are very cruel, you know . . ."

"What happened last time?" I asked.

"There was a knifing or two," said Purvis. He wouldn't say more than that. When I asked him what kind of music they'd had on their last trip, he said, "Only a nigger with a drum."

"Hurry now," the Captain said. "Let them put on what they wish."

"He knows they won't put on anything by themselves," said Purvis in a low disgusted voice. Stout was picking up armfuls of the clothes and flinging them at the blacks who stood silently and impassively.

"Show them!" cried the Captain. "Teach them! Dress them!"

"Are they dead?" inquired the Spaniard in a piercing voice. "If they are dead, they are of no use to me!" The Captain joined in his laughter, the sounds of which seemed to me unreal, as those of men imitating roosters.

With his outstretched arms, Ben Stout was supporting a man so bent I thought, for a second, the Captain had been fooled into shipping an ancient halfway around the world. Then Stout began to shake him. I saw his face. I realized he was no more than seventeen or eighteen years old. With one hand, Stout held the young man upright; with the other, he drew a woman's loose white gown over his head. The hem fell just below his knees.

I heard Sharkey laugh and Smith snicker. John Cooley said, "Why she's a pretty little thing, ain't she?" The Spaniard whispered to his servant. The black man stepped forward and opened his mouth. No sound issued forth. He waved his hands—he lifted clothes from the deck—he made as if to dress himself in them. His mouth remained open like a small dark empty cave where nothing lives. He dropped the clothes he was holding on the deck. When he stepped back to take his place behind the Spaniard, the slaves picked up the various garments scattered around their feet. I was no more able to fathom their expressions as they dressed themselves than I could have explained how the mute man had persuaded them to dress at all. There was not a scrap of cloth left on the deck. The slaves were like statues. The sailors moved among them, straightening a collar, rearranging a shawl, yanking down a shirt. One woman had not troubled to put her arms into the sleeves of the dress she had put on, and Cooley wound them about her neck and tied them in a knot. I saw the young black boy move to the rail, a thin white undergarment floating from his shoulders.

The rum keg was tapped, and the seamen began to drink clumsily and with gulping haste. Captain Cawthorne cried, "Don't neglect our guests!" Sharkey, whose arm the Captain had grabbed, looked at him in astonishment. When Sharkey gestured toward the Spaniard, the Captain hit him several times with considerable violence, all the while smiling as though they had been speaking together about pleasant matters. Sharkey was utterly bewildered. Cawthorne made him fill a cup of rum, guided his arm toward a black woman, then pushed the sailor's hand against the woman's mouth. "Our guests!" shouted the Captain. The woman coughed as she swallowed the burning stuff. "Bollweevil!" cried the Captain. "You'll dance us all now!"

I played my tunes. I could not hear my piping above the thumps of the sailors' boots and the slap of the slaves' feet. At first, I kept my eyes on the Captain who moved among his crew and cargo like a diving bird among a school of fish. He was dreadfully graceful and quick, so fast with his feet he could have danced for pennies on the riverside. Yet he had energy left over to pinch and hit and slap and punch the slaves and sailors alike. Purvis kept out of his way, but Stout, who'd drunk a good deal of rum by then, seemed to place himself in Cawthorne's way on purpose, roaring with laughter each time the Captain hit him.

The smell of rum was powerful. The slaves were drinking it avidly as though to assuage an endless thirst. The seamen drank to become merry but they only grew drunker. They clutched the slaves, they grabbed them by their waists, they hung on to their arms and flung them about, they fell upon them and dragged them to the deck. A few children suddenly broke away. I watched them run toward the bow.

They hid near the anchor where they huddled together like nestlings. Then I dropped my fife, whether because the dance had grown more frantic and abandoned and I was frightened, or whether I had become exhausted, I don't know. It rolled toward the rail.

It rolled! I felt the ship rocking ever so slightly. At the same instance, I felt a breeze.

"Look!" howled the Spaniard. All dancing stopped at that loud cry. The dazed sailors stared off in every direction. The Spaniard's servant was waving his hands slowly back and forth. His mouth was open, forming a dark circle.

"He sees a sail!" the Spaniard cried.

"A sail . . ." said someone.

"Stout!" called the Captain.

Stout staggered to the starboard side of the ship. I could see with what effort he was holding himself upright. The breeze suddenly doubled in force. I saw Purvis rise from where he'd been lying and look about himself as though mystified.

"An English ship," Stout declared. "I know her. She won't bother us in these waters."

"Get that Spanish flag down, Cooley," ordered the Captain.

At that moment, I heard Porter cry out from aloft, "A sail! Starboard side!"

The Captain looked straight up at the heavens. The scorn in his face would have singed a harder man than even he was. "Indeed, Porter!" he said softly. At that moment, one of the black men began to spin slowly on the deck, his arms held out like wings, turning, turning, until he fell and lay as if dead. Cawthorne said to me, "Stay by the children," and started aft. "Stout," he called over his shoulder. Stout stumbled after him. "I want the American flag hoisted."

"I know that ship, Captain," protested Stout. "She won't bother us."

"Cease!" snarled Cawthorne. "Do you hear that, you drunk hog?"

Stay by the children? I looked around wildly for Purvis. The breeze was becoming a wind which rose out of the darkness, then fell like a wave and scattered itself to every part of *The Moonlight*.

I heard Cawthorne say, "I don't trust your judgment, Stout, any more than I'd trust the British to do what they're supposed to. Get the niggers to the rail!" He sniffed the air. "There's something coming up that isn't English," he said.

"The hatch covers must go over," Stout said thickly. "And the leg restraints." A great moan suddenly went up from the slaves, and I saw Curry dumping the cauldron over the side.

What happened next took place so quickly that afterwards I could recall only fragments like pieces of dreams that sometimes haunt my waking hours. Through it all, most of the crew worked on the sails, and I glimpsed them from time to time as they climbed and clung to the rigging like great ragged moths. The American flag was hoisted. The Spaniard snatched up the Spanish flag from the deck where it had fallen. Stout, who vanished for a moment, reappeared, his hands full of shackles which he flung into the sea. Then Isaac Porter, down from his lookout perch, began to cry urgently in words that were not clear for the wind suddenly intensified its force, the sails smacked into position and the clatter of the anchors drowned out nearly everything. I saw the Spaniard raise his hands in apparent protest as the ship, with a great lurch, got underway. And his servant's hat suddenly blew off and spun away into the black night. Then Porter cried out again. "Boats!" I heard.

I saw Cawthorne rush to the rail, Stout at his side.

"By God!" Cawthorne thundered. "I see the ship! I see it. *It's American!* You disaster, Stout! You've murdered me! Get the slaves over! Get them over!"

I cried out in terror myself as I saw the luminous crest of a wave in the darkness, and right behind it on the next crest, a number of small boats coming directly at us, the rowers bent against the wind. At that moment, Sam Wick picked up a black woman and simply dropped her over the side. With hardly a pause, he then kicked over two men.

Now the slaves, aware of their mortal danger, sank down, piling themselves up on one another as though in this way they could protect themselves. They scratched the deck frantically as the seamen ran among them, grabbing them up and shoving them to the rail. I saw Cawthorne himself seize a small woman, lift her up and drop her into the sea. As he turned from the rail, three black men moved unsteadily toward him, flailing the air with their arms as though he were a wild animal. Cawthorne instantly drew his pistol and fired it directly into the face of one of the blacks. I fled to the bow, the shot echoing in my head. The storm suddenly broke, the sails tautened, and the ship gave a mighty shake. I could no longer see the small boats form the American ship. I could make out the Captain now standing by Purvis at the helm while all around them the seamen whipped the blacks over. I began to wail like a demented person, pleading with the small boats to catch up with us, to seize us. Then I heard children weeping. They were only a few feet away from where I stood, clinging to the young black boy who looked at me with such defiance I flung up my arms and shook my head violently to show I meant no harm. I heard running feet. Seth Smith passed me as I squeezed myself against the cathead. He found the children. The black boy struck him with his fists and his feet, but Smith ignored the blows and picked up the little ones and flung them off the bow. I screamed. Smith turned a mad face at me, his eyes glittering.

"Get to it!" he shouted crazily. I thought I saw pale giant sails suspended off the starboard side like a curtain dropped form heaven, but *The Moonlight* lurched forward again, and the sails vanished as had the small boats. The black boy slipped behind the mast. We were still alive here, but in the sea, slaves and rowers were falling into the silent dark depths. Smith began to beat the air with his fists. I realized he was waiting for me to say something, do something. I stuck my foot in a coil of rope, then made as if I was trapped. "My foot's caught!" I cried. Smith ran off. I hastened to the boy who was clinging to the mast. I took hold of one arm, but he shook me off. His breathing had a dire sound to it, and I thought he might die of sheer terror. I took hold of him again, determined to hold on no matter how he struggled. Suddenly he gave way. I felt his breath fluttering against my face. I released his arm then, and motioned in the direction of the forehold. Then I got down on my hands and knees. He did the same. We crawled along beneath the main staysail that strained above our heads. I heard the Captain's shouts but not what he said. The wind howled.

We gained the hold and dropped down into it. In the dark, I found the boy's arm again. We went as far as we could from the open hatch. Between a nearly empty cask and the great root of the foremast, we crouched. Our breaths mingled. The boy whispered something. "I don't know," I said. He was silent. Then, to my horror, I saw the solid hatch cover descend over the hold, remembering at the same moment that the hatches were always closed in foul weather.

The hideous stench made breathing difficult. My legs began to cramp and every bone in my body ached. Something furry brushed against my hand. I got to my feet, cracking an elbow as I rose. The boy got up too, and we stood for a long time. I felt the ship heeling over as though a giant hand were pressing her to her side. Sometimes we sat, sometimes I dozed. Once, the boy took my hand and pressed it against the cask. I felt moisture. He directed my damp fingers to my mouth and I licked them. We took what wet we could, our fingers crossing the surface of the cask like moles. When the ship yawed, we were flung back against the timbers. Sometimes we clung to the cask to keep from landing on our heads. But as terrible as the storm was, it would be worse when the hatch was opened and we were discovered. I thought of Stout's face, how he would look, how he would smile when he saw us.

The boy spoke to me. I answered. Neither of us knew what the other said, but the sound of our voices in the dark held back dread as the thunderous violence of the storm broke all around us. There were moments when I wanted only to give way, to become a noise, a thing, so as not to *know* the terror I was feeling. We plunged and pitched through the sea—I know the ship made great speed those first hours, but it was the uneven lurching speed of a crippled runner.

We both slept. What I sensed as a long time grew immeasurable. These could not be hours passing, but days. As I sat, braced against the howling, crashing chaos above, taking some comfort from the small but steady sound of the black boy's breathing as he slept, I couldn't imagine night and day, dark and light, only the storm, the ship plunging through it like those stars I'd seen fall through heaven in late summer.

Once I woke to hear him crooning to himself. God knows what his words meant! But the sound of them! It will be like that, the last sound of the last soul on this earth. I shook his arm to make him stop and he laughed. It was then I felt a pang of hunger and remembered the biscuits Cawthorne had given me. We each had two. Though damp, they were fine biscuits and did not require to be broken by hammer.

We often held our strange conversations, each waiting for the other to finish as though we actually understood. Once, there was a terrible crash above. A violent shudder passed through the ship and entered my bones. I waited for the sea to rush over us. But it didn't come. And all the while, I scratched my legs frantically where the salt damp was biting my skin.

Then, long after we'd finished the last of the biscuits, at a time when I'd lost all sense of whether I was awake or dreaming, the hatch cover disappeared as though lifted by a mighty hand. I saw daylight. I saw a gray turbulent sky stirred by the wind. The boy and I looked at each other. In his sunken eyes, I saw the questions that must have been in my own.

I crawled among the casks until I found a piece of the rope ladder which still hung down from the deck. As I gripped it, water the color of the sky rushed into the hold and tossed me back to where I'd started as if I'd weighed no more than a gull's feather. I heard canvas flapping, the creaking of straining wood. I went back and took hold of the rope again and pulled myself up to the deck.

The first thing I saw was the ship's small boat smashed to bits. The mainmast lay athwart the deck, broken and twisted, its sails all rags. Beneath it lay Purvis, One leg free of the mast and floating in the water that advanced and retreated. The ship was awash to the hatches—the great wheel which had guided us such distances was now useless, floating among the ship's debris. Only the mizzenmast still stood, its sails whipping back and forth. I was drenched instantly. I rolled myself to Ned's bench and clung to it.

The water stung my eyes and filled my ears. It came again and again across the deck as the ship, slack and lifeless, rose and crashed down. Nothing stood still in all the gray bawling world.

I raised myself up and flung myself across the bench. Through my blurred sight I caught a glimpse of what I could not believe was there. Land! But even as I drew breath, the ship plunged down into a trough between giant waves. When it rose, I saw palm trees, their topmost branches combing the sky as though on the very point of being yanked out of the earth and carried heavenward. I had never felt such fear—no storm in the great ocean was so awful as this—to see land, to be so near the shore . . .

I heard a moan, muffled like the cry of a sea bird in a heavy rain. I raised my head then ducked as a wall of water rushed toward me. I felt the weakness of my fingers gripping the soaked wood of Ned's bench. Then I saw Benjamin Stout caught like a huge fly in a tangled web of rope. He stared blindly at the sky. Another wave came across the deck. I looked for Stout. He was gone along with all the rope which had trapped him. I saw land again. I made out the foam crests of the waves breaking against the shore, and I cursed the light that let me see. If it had only been dark!

It must have taken an hour for me to move my hands to the bench leg, to lower myself through the battering wind to the deck. Coughing, unable to see, I felt my way back to the hold. Inch by inch, I advanced. Once I grabbed at something only to feel it give softly in my fingers, the feel of cloth and bone and flesh traveling up my arm. I shouted with horror and my mouth filled with water. I choked and sputtered and tried to see whose leg I had grabbed. I thought it was Cooley but could not be sure. I thought I heard a cry for help but the wind mimicked distress so perfectly there was no way to tell. The ship hit the bottom of another trough just as I reached out and took hold of the rope. I could not move. It was hopeless. I had no strength left to brace myself against the elements which would soon send the ship and her cargo of corpses to the bottom, to the depth where no wind blew.

I felt a monstrous convulsion traveling through what was left of *The Moonlight*. I opened my mouth and shouted with all my might as though such a pitiful squeak, lost in the smash and crack of the wind and sea, could bring the storm to a halt. An instant later, the ship listed so far to her side it seemed that only the wind kept me plastered to the deck like a bug blown against a piece of bark. But the shudder had moved me forward a foot, and I was able now to fling myself over the edge of the hold.

My head and shoulders were hanging down into the darkness. I heard isolated *pings* of dripping water in the strange stillness below the deck. Then I saw something waving, something living. A dozen frights rushed through my mind until sense came back to me and I knew it was the black boy reaching up. I gripped his fluttering fingers. Then, as I edged myself down, his arm came to guide me.

Squatting, we held each other's arms. He was trembling, as I was. He spoke to me. I gripped him more strongly and nodded. A wave hit. We fell and rolled among the casks, holding on to each other as we gathered bruises and splinters. We lay against the hull in a pool of warmish water that had its own small tides as the ship rocked back and forth.

Then, gradually, the pounding on the deck grew less; the wind receded; the rattling and thumping of the ship's gear—the very stuff of the ship herself—diminished to a low quarrelsome mumble. There were little easings and movements I barely noticed through the hull. I realized the ship was settling upon something, a reef, a rock, something upon which it would rest briefly before plunging to the bottom. The boy took my wrist. I felt rather than saw the motion of his hand as he gestured toward the hatch.

We made our way to the deck. It was nearly dark. Waves washed placidly across the ship. I could see the shore now, the narrow beach, the line of palms. I glanced at the boy. He was gazing intently at the shore, his mouth slightly open, a look of eagerness on his face. Did he think we had come to his home? I caught his arm and shook my head. The light left his face. I wondered if we were looking at Cuba.

Then I nearly jumped out of my skin. A wild choking laugh erupted from what was left of the aft quarters. I heard the distinct sound of a bottle smashed against wood. Cawthorne was not dead.

The laugh ended abruptly. There was only the soft gathering rush of water, the hush beneath the dying wind. The boy gestured toward the shore. We slid down the deck, bracing our feet against what was left of the main rail. A piece of the boom lay close. I touched the boy, and pointed at the length of wood. We worked away at it, disentangling it from the sail that was wound around it. I could not estimate how far we were from the shore. But I knew we'd drown if we stayed on the ship.

I heard another shout. Cawthorne lay against the mizzenmast, the angle of the ship such that he was nearly horizontal. I thought he had seen us, but no. His gaze passed over us without recognition. Perhaps he could see nothing. I looked back at the water. I could only swim like a dog. It was the way I'd learned. I didn't know if it would carry me—pawing—all that way. And I didn't know if the boy could swim. But what choice was there?

We flung the piece of boom into the water and slid in after it. I lost sight of the boy almost at once. My lungs took in water. I sank. A hand touched mine. I rose sputtering. He was there, his head bobbing a few feet away. We managed to take hold of the wood, and kicking our feet, we made for the shore.

I turned my head once. I saw, against the cloud streaming sky now streaked with an earthen glow, the Captain, his hand clawing the air. The ship was sinking slowly from view. For an instant, I felt a twinge in my ear as though Cawthorne's teeth had closed upon it once again. I wondered if, with all the brandy I was sure he'd taken, he'd know the difference between breathing air and water.

I don't know how we reached the shore which had looked so close yet ever receded as we swam toward it. The darkness came down all at once like a thick black cloth. I don't remember when we lost the boom, how often we reached toward each other and found only the water, or how many waves broke over us and lifted us to terrifying heights.

How long it took us, I'll never know. But even now I can feel the urgency of our struggle, the hope that delivered me from the depths and brought me up to air again and again as though most of my true life had taken place in that stretch of sea.

The Old Man

WHEN WE AWOKE, it must have been in the first light of morning. The tranquil sea was turning from gray to a mild blue as the sun's pale rays spread out over the water.

I breathed in the land smells, earth and trees and the sharp salty aroma of sea wrack.

But chickens! I suspected my own hunger had made me imagine I smelled them. I lay still, grateful for the thin warmth of the sun. Something ran across my ankle. It tickled, and I sat up and saw a crab no bigger than my thumb. The boy, still dressed in the woman's undergarment, lay a few feet away. He was sniffing the air.

"Chickens?" I wondered aloud. The boy said a word in his own language and smiled. We got up, both of us brushing off patches of sand that had dried on us. He started to pull off the garment when something caught his attention in the long defile of palms above the beach. I looked. Behind the palms was the thick dark green of what appeared to be impenetrable underbrush. There was no wind at all, only a great stillness.

Chickens! It was no imagining. Out from the trees, bobbing its head as it clucked came a large yellow hen. *People*, I thought. My knees began to tremble. That feathered lump meant farm and man, and I was afraid.

I stood poised for flight, waiting for the chicken's owner to make his appearance, armed with pistol and whip—God knows what else! The chicken scratched the sand. I grabbed the boy's arm and pointed down the beach. But he continued to stare at the creature as it advanced in our direction. Suddenly he grabbed up a stone, then looked at me inquiringly. How I wanted to nod yes! It was such a plump chicken! But I shook my head vigorously and waved at the trees. He took my thought and dropped the stone, then he hitched up the skirt of the undergarment and we started off down the beach. We had nearly gained the point, when a voice called out, "Stop!"

But we kept right on going until we were on the small neck of land and could see to the other side. I saw with dismay that there was no beach, only a line of steep-faced rocks covered with hair-like ferns. We stopped dead. There was no place to go except into the water. Dreading what I would see, I turned. To my astonishment, an elderly black man stood watching us from near the place where we had slept, and where I could still make out the faint outlines of our bodies in the sand. Beside him was his harbinger, the yellow hen, her head cocked. She grabbed up something, and I guessed it was the crab which had so recently ascended my ankle.

I looked at the boy. His face was radiant. But the glow was gone almost instantly. He must have realized that although the old man's clothes were ragged, they were those of white men.

The old man began to come toward us with slow steps. We went to meet him. I could not think what to say, how to explain the circumstances which had brought us to this shore. I wished the boy and I had landed on one of those uninhabited islands Purvis had told me about—out of the reach of others—for I found a bottomless distrust in my heart for anything that walked on two legs. It was the old man who broke the silence.

"Where you going? Where you come from?" He looked at me quickly, then away. I observed how carefully he began to study the black boy. Then, when I hadn't answered, not being able to find words, he said, "Well, master?"

"No!" I croaked. "I'm not his master."

The old man reached out and took the boy's arm and turned him around. Then he pulled the woman's garment off him. He touched some old scars on the boy's back.

"Our ship sank in the storm," I said. "We swam to shore."

The old man nodded and released the boy. "Where are the others?" he asked.

"There was the crew," I said. "They drowned." I looked out at the sea. There was nothing.

Everything marched at dead measure. The sun's heat had grown stronger, and I was suddenly aware of my thirst.

"We haven't eaten for a long time," I said. "We've had no water, either, and we don't know where we are."

"You in Mississippi," said the old man, looking at the boy. "He don't say nothing. Why is that?"

"He speaks his own language," I replied, wondering if we would, at least, get something to drink. There must be food and drink there in the forest. The old man had come from *some* place. "But he's not learned our language yet," I added.

"Our language . . ." echoed the old man.

"My name is Jessie Bollier," I said desperately. The old man seemed to be weighing us, deciding . . .

"What's his name?" he asked.

I touched the black boy's hand. He tore his gaze away from the old man. I pointed to myself. "Jessie," I said. Then I pointed to him. "Jessie?" he questioned.

"What's your name?" I asked the old man. He looked out at the water. He would not find a trace of *The Moonlight*. During the night, it must have been carried off whatever had held it up and was now resting on the bottom. He had not answered my question. I turned again to the boy, pointed at myself and repeated my name. Then I touched his shoulder. This time he said clearly, "Ras!"

I walked away from him. "Ras!" I called. "Jessie," he answered.

The old man made up his mind. "You come with me now," he said. He walked up toward the palms, grabbing up the chicken without changing his pace. It squawked with rage. We followed. There was nothing else we could do. He might give us something to drink.

I would not have imagined there was anything like a path in the forest, but there was, just a slight indentation wide enough for a foot. The old man kept looking back at the boy. He took special care to see we were not whipped by the close growing branches, holding them until we had passed. He led us for perhaps a quarter of a mile, then halted for no apparent reason and dropped the hen to the ground. She ran off into a thicket, clucking indignantly.

"She go where she pleases," said the old man. "I spared her so far."

Then with both hands, he grabbed up a great thatch of branches and thrust it aside. To my surprise, a large clearing was revealed. In the center was a small hut and a few yards of spaded earth and to one side, a pig pen, where a sow nursed a number of piglets while a giant pig grunted and rolled in the mud. A few chickens scratched in the dirt. The old man led us to a large cask nearly full of water. He handed a dipper full to Ras, then held the boy's hand and pressed it and said softly, "Slow, slow . . ."

Ras finished and held out the dipper to me. At the first taste of the dank cool water I forgot all else and drank steadily until the old man shook me and drew me away from the cask. "That's enough," he said.

He took us into his hut. The earth floor was hard and smooth. I saw a crude hearth with a few blackened pots and utensils grouped around it. A tree trunk served as a table. On the floor, there was a bed of straw and leaves.

I sank to the floor, resting my back against the wall. Ras remained standing, watching the old man set out food for us on the tree-trunk table.

On land at last, in a silence broken only by insects chirring, warmed by the damp breathless heat of the forest around us, resting on a surface that remained steady, about to assuage my hunger, I couldn't understand the heaviness that weighed me down, that made it so difficult to breath. I wanted—and this made me wonder if I'd really lost my wits—to be dropped in the mud with the pig outside, to roll in the wet dirt, to bury myself in it. I wanted to cry.

How soon before the bodies of the crew would be washed up on the sand? Would I look once more at Ben Stout's face drying out in the sun? I felt again the violent heaving water through which Ras and I had struggled to the shore. How had I done it with my dog's pawing? Suddenly, I heard an inner voice crying out "Oh, swim!" as it had whenever I'd thought of my father sinking among the dead drowned trees in the Mississippi River. I wondered if it was that plea that had served me so well at last.

A few days later, when Ras and I and the old man were walking on the beach, we found a few things from *The Moonlight*, Ben Stout's waterlogged Bible, pieces of Ned Grime's bench and many odd pieces of wood which the old man gathered and piled up out of reach of the tide. I found, drying out in the sun and buzzed over by small biting flies, a long piece of rope.

"You won't find nobody," the old man said to me. "The sharks will rack their bones. They don't leave nothing."

I was thinking of rope, how, leading up to the topmost sail, it had hummed with life, how, stretched and taut, it had guided or restrained the sails just as bridles and reins guide and restrain horses. I picked it up and waved away the cloud of insects. The rope smelled of decay.

I had not eaten much at our first meal, but I made up for that in the next few days. One night, the old man made a stew of okra and greens and ham. Ras and I ate until the food ran down our chins and we were covered with grease. He pointed at me and laughed. I drew my finger along his chin, showing him the ham fat that had collected on his cheeks. He laughed harder. It was still daylight. The birds were calling each other to sleep. The old man smiled—very slightly—and rose to light an oil lamp. I took the pot outside and scoured it with sand. Then Ras and I squatted near the hut. A huge beaked bird flew above us toward the dying light in the west. I heard from far off the great breathing of the sea, taken in, expelled. We sat there until dark when the bugs drove us inside.

Ras and I talked together, knowing we couldn't understand each other. Sometimes pointing to a tree or a bird or some feature of his face, he would slowly pronounce a word. I would repeat it, then say it in English. In this fashion we learned a few words of each other's languages. The old man had given us clothes, and though they didn't fit in a way that would have won my mother's admiration, we were at least dressed.

The old man was entirely dependent upon the little patch of ground he had planted and his few animals for the sustaining of his life. He was seldom idle. I wondered at some of the things he had in his hut, where they had come from. I knew by then he must be an escaped slave who had founded for himself this tiny place of liberty deep in the forest. Often I felt we were as remote from other people as we would have been on a deserted island.

At the end of the first week, the old man told me his name. A piglet had gotten out from under the fence. I chased it, crying "Old man! Old man!" He caught up with me in the thick undergrowth, swooped down on the piglet, saying at the same time, "You can call me Daniel."

I could tell by looking at Ras that we were both gaining weight. I began to feel the return of my strength. We rose at dawn and went to sleep with the birds. Daniel cautioned us not to go too far from the hut and to be careful and watch out for snakes. We brought to the hut the wood he'd collected on the beach, and we fetched water to keep the cask full from a nearby stream. There were always chores to be done. But there were games and idle times. We hid from each other and sought each other out; we built a small shelter out of fallen branches; we chased the chickens until Daniel stopped us. It was a time without measure in which no thought of the future intruded, when the memory of the past was put aside for a while.

One evening, Daniel rested his hand on Ras's head. The boy looked up at him questioningly. Daniel patted him gently. Watching them both from the doorway, I shivered.

The very next night, I learned what was to happen to Ras.

After we'd cleaned up the pots from dinner and Daniel had lit the lamp, I heard a footstep. The sow grunted. Daniel went outside. He spoke at some length to someone. Then he came back and said, "You be quiet, Jessie. I want you to sit outside. Here. Take this and wrap it around you against the bugs." He handed me a dusty cloak. I shook it out. A smell of mildew rose from its creases. "Don't look so scared, boy," said Daniel. "Nothing bad is going to happen to you."

Standing at the edge of the clearing were two black men. They watched me go to the pig pen and sit down against the fence, then they entered the hut. For a long time I strained to make sense out of the murmur of voices inside. I felt pitiful and alone, then the pig came and lay down behind me on the other side of the fence and grunted softly. I grunted back. It was better than talking to myself. I must have dozed for a while. I heard Daniel speaking from the doorway, "Come back now, Jessie."

When I entered the hut, I saw the two men had gone. Ras was squatting on the floor, his fingers tracing some design on it.

"What's going to happen?" I asked.

"We're going to get him out of here," he said. "We got a way of taking him north, far from this place. One of those men speaks his language. Look at him! See how he's thinking?"

Ras was looking at me now but I might as well have been invisible. He didn't *see* me at all.

"He's going to be all right," Daniel said as he sat on the straw bed. He was rubbing his ankle. Beneath his fingers, I caught a glimpse of an old scar.

"And me?" I asked.

"You got to go home to your family," he said. "You rested up now. It'll take you a few days walking."

"When is Ras—"

"He's going tomorrow soon as it gets dark. They coming for him."

Daniel got up suddenly and walked to where Ras was sitting. He took the boy's hand in his own.

"You be all right," he said over and over again in a kind of lullaby.

On our last morning together, Ras and I went down to the beach. We found, resting amid the sea wrack at the high water line, a curved piece of the ship's bow.

Ras was quiet, given to long silent staring pauses when he stopped whatever he was doing and went off into a private vision of his own. We stayed close to each other all that day.

Daniel made us a pudding of yams for supper. Ras had little appetite, but the old man kept heaping food on his plate with a pleading look on his face. I saw Ras try; he knew he had to eat.

At dark, one of the two men came back. Daniel had made a packet of food which he gave to Ras. He had dressed in clothes the man had brought him and they fitted him well. I wondered to whom the clothes belonged, and where *he* was. Ras looked taller—almost unknown. He and the young man who'd come to fetch him spoke infrequently. Whatever would happen to him now, Ras was resolved, tight with intention. I could tell it by the way he determinedly stuck his narrow feet into black boots, the way he took the food from Daniel's hands, the way his glance rested constantly on the doorway. Daniel bent over him. I saw Ras's arms slide around his back, his hands resting on the old man's shoulders. Then he came to me.

"Jessie?" he said.

I nodded, uneasy under the expressionless stare of the young man.

"Nose," said Ras as he touched my nose.

I smiled then. He placed a finger against my front teeth.

"Teef," he said.

"Teeth," I corrected.

Ras laughed and shook his head. "Teef," he said again, and then, gravely, "Jessie."

He was gone in an instant. Daniel and I were alone.

I felt such a hollowness then, and the awakening of the memory, asleep these last weeks, of the voyage of *The Moonlight*. My mouth went dry. I sat on the floor and hid my head in my arms.

"Come here," said Daniel.

I looked up. He was sitting on his straw bed. I got up and went to him.

"Now, sit down, Jessie. And tell me the whole story of that ship."

I told him, leaving out nothing I could remember, from the moment when Purvis and Sharkey had wrapped me in that canvas to the moment when Ras and I had slid into the water from the sinking ship.

When I had finished, the old man said, "That's the way it was," as though everything I had described was only what he already had known.

I wanted to ask him if he too had come in that same way to this country, but something held me back. I asked him nothing.

"That boy, he be safe soon," said Daniel. "Now you go to sleep. You need your rest. You got to start before light. Listen, boy!" He stopped speaking and looked at my face intently. The lamp was low, and now the hut was like a clearing in the forest lit only by the last burning twig of campfire. The shadows deepened the sockets of his eyes. He seemed very old.

"If you tell your people about Daniel," he said, "Daniel will be taken back to the place he run away from. Are you going to tell them?"

"No, no!" I cried. I yearned to show him my resolve as though it were a thing like a shoe or a hoe that I could put in his hand.

"All right," he said. I couldn't tell if he believed me or not.

He woke me before the birds began their twittering. I dressed in the dark in the clothes he had given me. But I had no boots. He said, "You wrap your feet in these rags. They make it easier for you to get through the woods."

I bound my feet with the strips of cloth he handed me.

"Now listen sharp. I'm going to tell you how you get home."

Slowly, often stopping to make me repeat what he had said, he drew a chart of words that would lead me home to New Orleans.

I looked out into the woods. It was utterly dark.

"Here," said Daniel, as he handed me a packet.

"Something to eat," he said. I heard a grunt from the pig pen, a few squeals form the piglets, a drowsy cluck from a hen.

"Thank you, Daniel," I said.

"I hope you have a safe journey," he said.

I wanted him to touch my head as he had Ras's. But his arms remained unmoving at his sides. I looked into his face. He didn't smile. The distance between us lengthened even as I stood there, listening to his breathing, aware of a powerful emotion, gratitude mixed with disappointment. I thought of Purvis.

"Go on, now," he said.

I stepped out of the hut. Daniel had saved my life. I couldn't expect more than that.

Home and After

I WAS FRIGHTENED in the woods, in the dark. The path was no more than a tracing on the thick underbrush. With my bound feet, I often had to stop and feel around with my fingers until I found it again. In my wake, birds woke with sharp cries and complaints. The dawn's light was still too weak to penetrate the forest, although when I looked straight up, I could see the paling of the sky.

I was caught between the urge to move as rapidly as I could and to stay right where I was until daylight. What I dreaded, what turned my forehead damp with sweat, was a vision of snakes beneath the brush, snakes like strings of wet brown beads, or thick like the weathered gray hafts of axes, or brilliantly colored like precious stones.

Then I came to Daniel's first marker, a small clearing near a trickle of stream where someone had recently built a fire. The smell of the ashes had been revivified by the morning dew. I was comforted as though I'd met someone whom Daniel and I knew.

When the sun had risen to its zenith, I came to a rutted road where farm wagons had left their wheel tracks. The forest had thinned to a few sparse clumps of trees, and I saw the sea glittering a quarter of a mile away. Once, as I was crossing a scraggy meadow, I startled a small flock of brown birds which rose like an arch beneath which I glimpsed a great white sail on the sea. I wondered what sort of ship she was—and what she carried in her holds.

In the later afternoon, I passed through a marsh where I was sur-rounded by loops and circles of still water on the surface of which floated patches of flowers, and where long-legged birds gazed down at their reflections with grave looks. I was the only human being abroad. The sky seemed immense.

That night, I ate a portion of the food Daniel had prepared for me, and made myself as comfortable as I could in an abandoned wagon, its shaft aimed at the sky. I felt like a fool, but before climbing under it I had tossed stones at it to frighten away the snakes I was sure were nesting there.

Daniel's markers drew me through the second day—one was a curious pile of stones on each one of which was painted a human figure; another was a tiny gray cabin far off at the edge of a field. There was nothing to shelter me that night. I simply lay down on the ground. Before daylight, I was awakened by the soft close chittering of some little field animal which ran right across my chest.

On the third morning, I woke to mist and heat. The wagon ruts had disappeared. Instead, at regular intervals as though they'd been embroidered, were the distinct shapes of horses' hooves. On my left, the fields ran down to the sea where they ended at low sand hills. On my right were woods but these were tamed woods, more like a vast park. A low stone wall ran along the side of the dirt road. I followed along it until I came to the place where two tall columns marked the beginning of another road which ran straight as a plumb line to the steps of a great plantation house. A small lizard the color of blood ran up one of the columns, then stopped and played dead.

Splendid flowers bloomed along that road. The wide porch of the house was empty. Not a leaf moved in the windless air. Then, all at once, a man on a black horse rode into view. He halted. The horse pawed the ground then flung up its head. At that, as though summoned by the horse, three black men ran to the rider and helped him dismount. They dashed before him up the steps to open the doors while a fourth man led away the horse.

I forgot I was in full view—as they were. I saw the doors close behind the rider. The windows reflected nothing. There was no sign of life. The lizard ran down the column. I felt frozen, choked, as I had that first time on *The Moonlight* when I'd been summoned by Captain Cawthorne to dance the slaves. Then I heard a dog bark from far away, and I bounded down the road like a rabbit that has regained control of its limbs.

Later, the sky turned the color of soot. The rain began, slowly, hesitatingly, until the sky opened up and the water fell in sheets. I sheltered beneath a hedge, soaked through, watching the road turn to mud. I knew I could not be far from home now. To my dismay, I felt I could go no further. The water blinded me. It roared in my ears. I was filled with an apprehension that had no reasonable shape in my mind. It spread around me like a dark sea. I did not think my legs would move when I wished them to. Suddenly, moved by an obscure impulse, I held my breath. Somewhere, someone had once told me that there were people who could choke off their lives by an act of will. I toppled sideways and lay exposed to the rain. But I was breathing. I couldn't not breathe.

At twilight, the rain stopped and the sky cleared. From every blade of grass, from every leaf, hung glittering drops. My spirits revived. I tore off the rags from around my feet and continued down the road, mud oozing between my toes. I was hungry now but hunger didn't surprise me as it might have once. I slept that night in a fishing boat upturned on a narrow beach bordering an inlet. The last morning of my journey, I was awakened to bright sunlight by small buzzing flies.

By late afternoon, I was walking down Chartres Street toward Jackson Square. I looked like a muddy scarecrow but I didn't attract much attention, only a warning look from a lady sliding along beneath her parasol, and a vague smile from a riverboat captain who, having long since begun his day's drinking, allowed everything strange to amuse him.

I opened the door to our room as I had done in my imagination a hundred times. I took my first step inside. I heard a shriek, a cry. Betty and my mother and I stood silently for a moment, then we ran toward each other with such force I felt the little house shake in all its boards and bricks.

We talked through half the night. I learned of their frantic search which had followed my disappearance, how even that very day my mother had questioned venders in the market as she had done every day since I'd been gone. My mother often wept, not only because I, whom she'd thought dead, had been returned to her, but at the story of *The Moonlight*. When I described how the slaves had been tossed into the shark-filled waters of Cuba, she covered her face with her hands and cried, "I can't hear it! I can't bear it!"

It did not take long, to my surprise, for me to slip back into my life as though I'd never left it. There were signs—brooding looks from my mother, Betty's way of speaking softly to me as though I was an invalid, and, most startling, the change in Aunt Agatha who treated me now with affection and never called me a bayou lout. My mother guessed that the shock of my disappearance had changed her into what she had once been, a slightly soured but not bad-hearted woman. I was back in my life, but I was not the same. When I passed a black man, I often turned to look at him, trying to see in his walk the man he had once been before he'd been driven through the dangerous heaving surf to a long boat, toppled into it, chained, brought to a waiting ship all narrowed and stripped for speed, carried through storms, and the bitter brightness of sun-filled days to a place, where if he had survived, he would be sold like cloth.

I found work on the Orleans Bank Canal which was to eventually connect New Orleans to Lake Pontchartrain. That might have kept me occupied and earning my keep for some time, but I grew restless and began to think about what profession would suit me, and what would be available to one who could not afford much schooling.

At first, I made a promise to myself: I would do nothing that was connected ever so faintly with the importing and sale and use of slaves. But I soon discovered that everything I considered bore, somewhere along the way, the imprint of black hands.

With the help of an acquaintance of Aunt Agatha's, I was finally apprenticed to an apothecary. It would be a different future from the one I had once envisaged when I had wanted to become a rich chandler.

When my apprenticeship was finished, I went north and settled in a small town in the state of Rhode Island. Eventually, I sent for Betty and my mother. We were out of the south, but it was not out of me. I missed the sharp sweet smell of fruit lying in the sun in the stalls of the great market, and I dreamed of the long muddy Mississippi and languorous green twilights and the old amber and apricot colored walls of the houses of the rich in the *Vieux Carré*. I knew that some part of my memory was always looking for Ras. Once, in Boston, I thought I really saw him, and I ran after a tall slender young black man walking along in front of me. But it was not he.

In the war between the sates, I fought on the Union side and a year after the Emancipation Proclamation in 1864, I spent three months in Andersonville, surviving its horrors, I often thought, because I'd been prepared for them on *The Moonlight*.

After the war, my life went on much like my neighbors' lives. I no longer spoke of my journey on a slave ship back in 1840. I did not often think of it myself. Time softened my memory as though it was kneading wax. But there was one thing that did not yield to time.

I was unable to listen to music. I could not bear to hear a woman sing, and at the sound of any instrument, a fiddle, a flute, a drum, a comb with paper wrapped around it played by my own child, I would leave instantly and shut myself away. For at the first note of a tune or of a song, I would see once again as though they'd never ceased their dancing in my mind, black men and women and children lifting their tormented limbs in time to a ready martial air, the dust rising from their joyless thumping, the sound of the fife finally drowned beneath the clanging of their chains.

Related Readings

from

Escape from the Slave Traders

Dave and Neta Jackson

This fictional story, written by Dave and Neta Jackson, is based on historical truths about two young African boys who are captured by slave traders. Like Jessie in The Slave Dancer, *Chuma and Wikatani are going about their daily chores when they are brutally snatched by these strangers.*

Red Caps in the Mist

"CHUMA! Chuma!"

The urgent call cut through the morning mists that floated along the shore of Lake Shirwa. *Why is Wikatani yelling at me again?* wondered Chuma. He thought the older boy bossed him around too much, especially so early in the morning. What was the hurry this time? They would get the village sheep to the pasture soon enough, well before the African sun rose high enough to drink the dew drops off the tender blades of grass.

"Chuma, help . . . !" And then Wikatani's voice was choked off as though he were gagging on a ball of wool. Chuma swung his staff at the heels of the last lazy sheep. The sheep leaped ahead to catch up with the flock that stretched around the bend of the lake shore and disappeared into the mist. *Wikatani is always in a hurry,* Chuma thought. *What difference does it make whether the sheep eat along the trail or in the pasture?* Still, he couldn't remember Wikatani's voice ever sounding so urgent.

Instead of trying to push his way through the flock of sheep, Chuma ran out into the shallows of the lake to get around the woolly animals. The cool water splashed high over his body with each step until he hit a hole and suddenly sunk in water up to his neck. Chuma was a good swimmer, and there was no danger, but he grabbed quickly at the folds of his clothes to make sure the yam he had hidden there for lunch was still safe. He also checked to see that his drinking gourd still hung from the cord around his neck.

He swam strongly until his feet touched bottom again, and he waded to shore. With a brief scramble that dislodged sand and gravel, he made it to the top of the bank and plowed through the tall grass to a point where he could again meet the trail. He paused to scan the trail and listen for Wikatani. Straight ahead of him, through the fog he thought he could make out his friend, but who were the strange men, and what was wrong?

Wikatani looked as if he were fighting for his life! One man held him securely from behind while another man tried to bind the boy's feet with cords. Frightened, Chuma barely held back a scream. What should he do? Should he rush to the attackers and try to free his friend or hold back until he figured out what was happening? Just then Wikatani must have bitten the hand of the man who held him because the man yelped, and Wikatani began yelling again: "Chuma! Chuma! Run for help!" Quickly the man clamped his hand back over Wikatani's mouth and looked at Chuma.

Chuma stared in disbelief and shock as the stranger's fierce eyes locked on him, but only for a moment. Chuma spun around to run back down the lake shore to their village—but he was not fast enough. A third man who had hidden in the tall grass jumped out and faced him with a spear pointed right at his heart. Chuma froze in his tracks before he noticed that the man's spear had no point and looked more like a sawed-off canoe paddle with the handle pointed toward him.

Chuma thought of diving into the lake; not many people could outswim him. But before he could move, the man poked him hard in the chest with the pointless spear. It did not cut, but pain shot through his bones. Chuma decided not to make a run for it. Then the man began speaking to him in a strange language and motioning with his pointless spear. Chuma understood that he was being ordered to join Wikatani and the two strangers, so he turned and slowly walked through the deep grass to the trail.

When Wikatani saw that Chuma had been captured, the older boy's shoulders sagged. One of the men quickly tied Chuma's feet and then left both boys sitting helplessly on the ground by the trail while the men spoke to each other in their strange language.

Swallowing his fear, Chuma studied the features of the unusual looking men. He had never seen anyone who wore bright red caps or pants or vests. He knew they weren't from his tribe, the Ajawa. And they didn't look like Manganja tribesmen either. Even though the Ajawa tribe had sometimes feuded with the Manganja, they were the only two tribes in the area. The Ajawa villages were primarily situated around Lake Shirwa, while most of the Manganja villages were to the west, near Mount Zomba. So who were they?

One of the men near Wikatani stood up and raised his pointless spear to his shoulder. He pointed it toward one of the sheep that was grazing along the trail. Suddenly the pointless spear made a terrible boom, and white smoke shot out of the end. Both boys cried out with the thunder, then opened their eyes. There lay one of their sheep—dead!—while the others ran off. That was bad. The village elders would be angry at the boys for having lost a sheep, but what if the strangers stole or killed the whole herd? Fear gripped Chuma's stomach.

And what about the stranger's awesome weapon? To Chuma, it looked like the pointless spear had killed the sheep without the stranger having thrown it. "Very powerful magic," Chuma whispered to Wikatani.

"They are guns. I have heard of them," said Wikatani. "They can kill from far away."

"Of course . . . guns," said Chuma. He did not like to admit it when Wikatani knew something he did not know, even though Wikatani was thirteen and he was only twelve years old.

Then Chuma was surprised to notice the man pick up a regular spear. He could see by its tribal markings that it was a Manganja spear. The man walked over to the dead sheep and wiped some of the sheep's blood on the spear. He broke the spear over his knee and brought the pieces back and threw them on the ground near Chuma and Wikatani. Then he ordered one of the other men to pick up the dead sheep and carry it over, too.

Seeing the other man obey his order convinced Chuma that this man was the leader of the group, maybe even a chief, though they were all dressed the same.

When the other man brought the sheep back, he let some of the blood drip on the sand and grass around the area where the boys were bound. Chuma did not understand these strange actions, but it was getting scarier by the moment. Were they performing some kind of magic?

Next, the leader grabbed the drinking gourd that hung by a thong from Chuma's neck. With one jerk he broke the thong and then smashed the gourd on the ground. Chuma stuck his chin out at the man defiantly. He could make another drinking gourd. He only carried the gourd with its fresh water because it was convenient when he was watching the sheep on the hills around Lake Shirwa.

But the man also ripped the family bracelets from Wikatani's arms and threw them to the ground not far from the broken gourd. He gave more orders. One man tied Chuma's hands behind his back while the other tied Wikatani's behind his back, and then they cut the cords on their legs.

Finally, the leader of the Red Caps started up the trail while the other two men prodded Chuma and Wikatani to follow. *Now what's happening?* thought Chuma with alarm. *They are not stealing our sheep; they are taking us!*

One of the men carried the dead sheep over his shoulder. It was still dripping blood on the trail as they walked. In a short distance, they turned off the main trail along the lake shore and marched west, away from the lake. The path was barely visible as it wound uphill through the thick grass toward the jungle.

Chuma looked back anxiously. The mist was lifting from the lake, and before they entered the jungle he could see its peaceful surface shining in the morning sun. Far back along the shore were wisps of smoke rising from their village. That was home, and they were being taken away. *No one will know where we are!* worried Chuma. *They won't even miss us until tonight when we don't return with the sheep. By then we'll be so far away that they will never find us!* Below, their sheep were wandering away from the trail along the lake front. Suddenly a hopeful thought came to him: *Maybe some sheep will wander home. Someone will certainly notice and know something is wrong and come looking for us. Or else,* and his spirits fell, *or else they'll just think we've been careless.*

As they entered the jungle, Chuma could no longer see the lake. The dew that had clung to the grass of the open fields now dripped like rain from the trees and vines overhead. Monkeys screeched and swung from limb to limb as the boys and their captors passed beneath. As the Red Caps hurried the boys along under the dark trees, Wikatani said in a hushed voice, "They had a Manganja spear. Do you think they are from the Manganja tribe?"

"I don't think so," answered Chuma. "Why would the Manganja take us away?"

"They're our tribe's old enemies."

"Yes," said Chuma, "but it is a disgrace to send others to fight your battles. These aren't Manganja, and we are only boys. What could be gained by capturing us?"

"Well, I am a chief's son," said Wikatani, lifting his head proudly. "Much trouble will come from attacking *me*. We are headed west into Manganja country. The Manganja must be behind this, and they will pay!"

"But the Manganja have no reason to attack us," said Chuma again.

At that point a Red Cap slapped Chuma on the back of the head so hard that he stumbled and fell. With his hands tied behind his back, he was unable to catch himself, and his face plowed into the dirt. Fortunately the ground was soft, and Chuma was not hurt. He quickly got up spitting bits of leaves and dirt from his mouth.

"No talking! Just march," shouted the Red Cap angrily, gesturing, and raising his hand as though to strike again. Chuma was as surprised that this man could speak their language as having been hit on the back of the head. *What'd I do? What's so wrong with talking?* Chuma wondered.

Wikatani said, "Don't hit him. He didn't do anything."

"I said, 'No talking,'" yelled the Red Cap again, this time at Wikatani. He spoke the boys' language well enough for them to understand him, but his accent was very thick. Then the Red Cap swung his gun at Wikatani like a club. Wikatani dodged out of the man's reach and hurried on up the trail. Chuma followed as quickly as he could.

By noon Chuma was feeling hungry and thirsty. Safely tucked in the folds of his loincloth was the small, cooked yam that his mother had set aside for him to eat while he herded sheep. He longed to take it out and eat it, but his hands were tied. Besides, he was afraid that the Red Caps would throw it away as they had his drinking gourd.

Plodding along the jungle trail, Chuma's thoughts kept returning to the house with its sturdy mud walls and thatched roof where he lived with his father and mother and three little sisters. He wanted to be brave, to face this difficulty like a man, like his father . . . but he kept thinking of his mother. *Who'll fix my food?* he wondered, even though he knew that wasn't his worst problem at the moment.

War Drums

As the sun dropped lower, its warm rays pierced the jungle roof only occasionally. But when they did, the golden beams sliced through the forest to turn various ferns a bright green or the trunk of a tree a rich, brick red.

Chuma no longer knew where they were. The country was turning hilly, and Chuma felt certain they were headed toward Mount Zomba, but he had never been this far west. Would they soon arrive at a Manganja village? He had no way of knowing, but he almost wished that they would. He was so tired he thought he would drop, and he was hungry.

Then suddenly, without any warning, they stepped out into a small clearing and the Red Caps stopped. It seemed to be their camp. There were two simple shelters made of palm branches under which supplies were piled high. And there were two other Red Caps already there, sitting near a smoldering fire while they smoked rolled leaves of tobacco.

The man carrying the sheep dropped it on the ground by the fire, and the leader gave more orders in the strange language. Soon the men by the fire butchered the sheep and put it on a spit over the fire to cook it.

The man who had slapped Chuma herded the boys over to the edge of the clearing and tied a rope tightly to each boy's ankle. The rope was also tied securely to a tree. He cut the cords that bound their wrists together, then left to join the others near the fire. Chuma and Wikatani tried to make themselves comfortable on the ground between the great roots of the tree and waited to see what would happen.

Nighttime in the jungle can be very dark; very little starlight makes its way through the dense roof of leaves. Even at the edge of the clearing it was dismally dark. Chuma and Wikatani sat dejectedly watching the five Red Caps around their small fire feasting on the roasted sheep and passing a jug of some sort of liquor. *Those men have no right to be eating our sheep!* Chuma thought angrily. Hunger kept him hoping that the Red Caps would bring them some of the mutton, but soon the men were so drunk they fell asleep.

With the pain mounting in his stomach, Chuma finally dug into the folds of his loincloth and pulled out the cold yam. He took a bite.

It was so good . . . or maybe it was just that he was *so* hungry. He took another bite, then nudged Wikatani: "Want some yam?"

"What?"

"You want a bite of my yam?" whispered Chuma.

"Where'd you get that?" said Wikatani, groping in the dark until he found the yam.

"My mother. It was wrapped in my clothes."

"I never knew a yam could be so good," Wikatani sighed, handing the remainder back to Chuma. "Do you think we can get these ropes off our ankles?"

"I don't know," said Chuma, taking another bite and then putting the rest of the yam back into his clothes. He went to work trying to wiggle his foot out to the loop that held it firmly. But the harder he pulled, the tighter the rope seemed to hold him. "I can't get it off."

There was a quiet moan from Wikatani. "I made it."

"Then help me."

Wikatani pulled and tugged. He used his teeth to try and tease the knot loose, but it was no use. The rope held Chuma fast to the tree.

"See if you can find something sharp to cut the rope," said Chuma.

Wikatani slipped off into the dark, and suddenly Chuma felt terribly alone. He waited a long time. *Wikatani ought to be back by now*, the boy thought, his heart beating fast. *Maybe he got lost. What if he never comes back?*

And then, as if he had never been away, Wikatani was at his side. "I can't find anything sharp. Only a few stones around here, and they're all smooth. I can't see a thing in this darkness."

"What about a knife from the Red Caps?" asked Chuma.

"Are you crazy? What if they woke up?"

They sat in silence for a while. Finally, Chuma said, "Maybe you should go for help."

"In the dark? I'd get lost for sure and the hyenas would find me."

It had been a bold suggestion, and Chuma shivered. The short time that Wikatani had been away had been enough to let him know how much worse it was to be a captive alone. But it seemed the only way. "How about just before it gets light? You could hide in the jungle until you can see and then find your way home."

"I guess so," admitted Wikatani. "But for now, let's get some sleep."

The constant chatter of jungle birds and monkeys woke Chuma. He had been dreaming about his three sisters playing at the edge of the lake. *Home. Home is so good,* he thought, and a heavy sadness spread through his heart when he remembered where he was.

A faint light tinged the sky above the clearing. They had slept longer than they should have! He shook Wikatani, and they both sat up. But in addition to the jungle noises, they could hear something else: the thump, thump, thumpity-thump of distant drums.

"Chuma, listen—Ajawa drums."

"You're right." Chuma imagined some of the head men of his village beating the hollow logs that sent their messages for miles through the jungle. Their rhythms could announce many things, but this beat meant . . . "War. It's war against the Manganja," concluded Chuma in a hoarse whisper.

"Because we're missing?" his friend asked.

"Maybe." Chuma thought for a moment. "That broken Manganja spear and the sheep's blood did make it *look* like the Manganja had captured us."

"And now Ajawa warriors will attack them."

"Yes. I think the Red Caps set it up that way. But why?" wondered Chuma out loud.

"Right now, who cares? I've got to get out of here."

"Take care," said Chuma, putting his hand on his friend's shoulder. "And come back soon. I don't like being a prisoner."

As Wikatani slipped away, Chuma could barely see him moving through the dense jungle as he tried to get around the campsite and find the trail by which they had entered the small clearing.

Then suddenly a terrible howling erupted. Wikatani must have come upon some baboons that were trying to raid the Red Caps' camp. The baboons screeched and yelled as they scampered up the vines to reach the safety of the trees.

Chuma held his breath and wished he could silence the baboons, but it was no use. Two of the Red Caps sat up and spotted Wikatani running down the trail. They grabbed their guns and tore down the trail after him.

"Run, Wikatani, run," urged Chuma under his breath, his fists clinched in fear. If Wikatani did not escape, they might not be rescued. And if they were not rescued, there might be a war, and many Ajawa would die.

Chuma wanted to pray to the spirits, but he knew the spirits didn't care. Their help could only be obtained by a sacrifice, and he had nothing to give. Then he remembered the small scrap of yam left from the night before. He dug it out. *It's my only food*, he thought. *If I throw it to the spirits, I might die. But if I don't, Wikatani might not escape.*

Before he could decide, a gun boomed in the distance. Chuma's heart sank. *Had the Red Caps killed Wikatani?* He waited but heard no more booms, just the sounds of the jungle coming alive in the morning—birds singing, insects buzzing, and still in the distance the talking drums.

When he felt he could wait no longer, he heard footsteps coming up the trail. The sight of Wikatani staggering back into camp was a tremendous relief. At least he was alive! One of the two Red Caps who followed him had cut a stiff vine and was using it to whip Wikatani every few steps if the boy did not move fast enough. The boy's arms were tied behind him. When they arrived at the tree where Chuma was tied up, the Red Caps gave Wikatani a shove that knocked him to the ground. The man was yelling at the boys in his strange language as he retied the rope around Wikatani's ankle, leaving some extra rope to tie around his other ankle, too. Then he gave Chuma's rope a big yank to see that it remained tight. Chuma's ankle throbbed with pain, the rope was so tight.

"What happened?" Chuma asked as the Red Cap went back to his camp. Then he realized what bad shape his friend was in. He was smeared with mud, and he had scratches and scrapes up and down both legs. There was a cut across his forehead that was oozing blood and beginning to swell. "What happened to you?" asked Chuma again anxiously.

"They caught me," pouted Wikatani, tears welling up in the corners of his eyes.

"I can see that," said Chuma. "But how?"

"I don't know," Wikatani said, looking away into the jungle. "I ran and ran. I knew they were behind me. I ran down a little hill and crossed a stream. I was climbing the other side when they shot at me with a gun. I did not want to die, so I stopped. When they caught me, they beat me."

Chuma asked no more questions.

By noon the Red Caps still hadn't given the boys anything to eat or drink. Chuma began to worry. He'd been thirsty before, but this was serious. His mouth was completely dry, and his tongue had swelled up so that he talked funny. His head felt light, as if he might fall over if he stood up. And Wikatani looked worse as the hours passed.

Finally, he decided they must do something, even if the Red Caps got angry. So he began to yell. "Give us food! We need water!" He knew that at least one of the men understood the Ajawa language. But when the Red Caps looked over at him, they just pointed and laughed. Still, Chuma kept yelling. Maybe their captors would get tired of the noise and give them what they needed.

One Red Cap grabbed a leg bone from the sheep they had feasted on the night before. Chuma eagerly saw that there were still some shreds of meat on it. The Red Cap walked toward the boys, and Chuma sat quietly in expectation. The Red Cap stopped a short distance away and gave Chuma a wicked grin. Then he dropped the bone to the ground, kicked dirt on it, and said, "Hungry?" When he made a gesture for Chuma to come get it, Chuma lunged, but the bone was out of reach. He pulled hard on the rope that bound him to the tree, got down on the ground and stretched out on his belly reaching as far as he could, but the bone was still beyond his reach.

The Red Cap broke into a great laugh, and the others joined in. The more Chuma stretched and groaned, the more the Red Caps roared until they were bored with their game.

But Chuma refused to give up in defeat. He crawled back to the tree and began looking around until he found a small stick. Then, attracting as little attention as possible, he scooted back toward the bone and reached out with the stick.

It just reached, and he began rolling the bone toward him. He got it rolled half way over, then it rolled back. He tried again, but just when it was about to come a full turn, he slipped and bumped it back—even farther away! After that, he could not reach it at all.

"Chuma, Chuma," Wikatani whispered. "Try this." It was a longer stick with a little branch on the end.

Using it like a hook, Chuma was able to roll the bone back and finally retrieve it.

Back at the tree, the boys eagerly pulled the remaining meat from the bone. It may have been too dirty even for the dogs back in the village, but they were so weak from hunger, they didn't even care. They ate it anyway, and it tasted good.

As Chuma was gnawing the last bit of gristle from the bone, Wikatani said, "Where did they go?"

In their excitement over having something to eat, the boys had not noticed that the Red Caps had left camp. "Ah, they're around here somewhere," Chuma said.

"I don't think so," said Wikatani. "I think they've left. Look. The supplies under that far shelter are missing. They've gone somewhere."

"Now's our chance!" said Chuma. "We've got to get free and get out of here!"

In Camp with the "Enemy"

Try as they would, the boys couldn't make the knotted ropes give. And soon the boys' hunger and thirst became a nightmare that overshadowed their desire to escape. Wikatani hurt everywhere from his beating, and his cuts were already infected. Chuma hated the thought of dying tied to a tree. He and Wikatani lay on the ground, weak with hunger, dehydration, and exhaustion. What seemed like an eternal day of torment finally blended into the night and the boys drifted off into a fitful sleep

In the middle of the night, something woke Chuma. At first he was confused. *What was happening?* Then he yelled, though the sound came out more like a squeak. "Rain! Wikatani! It's raining!"

Cupping their hands, the two boys caught the sweet water, satisfying their thirst again and again. The shower did not last long, and soon they were both asleep again.

The next morning the clearing was still deserted. "Are the Red Caps going to leave us here to die?" asked Chuma.

"No, they will come again," Wikatani assured Chuma. "Some of their supplies are still here."

The water had renewed their strength, but the hunger grew worse. As the day wore on, Chuma had a thought. He reached over and picked at the bark of the tree they were tied to. Then he began ripping off the bark as fast as he could. Termites! And grubs! *Why hadn't they thought of it sooner?* Wikatani helped him, and the boys popped the insects and little white grubs into their mouths as fast as they could. It took a lot of termites, but the terrible pain in their stomachs finally settled into a dull ache. Both boys hoped their meal stayed down, but it was not their last meal from the tree.

Two days went by before the Red Caps returned to camp with dozens of new captives. Men, women, and children were tied together with stout ropes. Many of the children were younger than Chuma and Wikatani. The Red Caps frequently hit the men with the butts of their guns and slapped the women and children. The younger children were wailing with fear.

The Red Caps cracked real whips this time, not just vines like they'd used on Wikatani. The whips whined through the air and cracked on bare skin, raising huge welts and sometimes cutting the skin open as the people were pushed into the center of the clearing.

Chuma and Wikatani stared open-mouthed. "Look!" Chuma whispered as he noticed the tribal markings tattooed on the bodies of the captives. "They're all Manganja."

"You're right. And some of the men are wounded."

"Not gun wounds . . . spear."

The boys watched as two of the Red Caps set to work attaching Y-shaped poles to the necks of the men. Each pole was about six feet long and branched into a Y at the end. The Red Caps put a Y around a man's neck and fastened it by driving a long metal spike through the tips of the open ends of the Y. This left the man with a huge pole sticking out in front, or to his side or back. It made any fast movements impossible because the poles had a tendency to catch on things, giving the wearer a sharp and painful jolt in the neck.

"They're making slaves of them!" Wikatani said in shock. "Those poles keep slaves from running away. No one can run through the jungle with one of those things around his neck." Just then one of the captured men spit on his captors after they'd put the Y on his neck and began kicking wildly. A Red Cap grabbed the pole and flung the man to the ground without getting close enough to be kicked or hit.

Chuma stared in awe. He, too, had heard of this practice for controlling slaves. In fact, once he had seen a thief treated this way as a punishment.

When the Reds Caps had attached Y-sticks to all the men, they set to work retying the frightened women together with strong ropes from one woman's neck to another's, creating a human chain.

Chuma counted a total of eighty-three captives. Several of the children couldn't be more than five years of age, and there were a few who were still in their mothers' arms. Some of the Manganja carried personal belongings—cooking pots, water gourds, and bags probably containing cornmeal or cassava root flour.

Many of the women were crying with grief and fear, their tears mingling with their children's who clung to them. But as evening approached some of the people began trying to make the best of their situation, arranging a family space to sit down and huddling everyone together. At first this activity created a great deal of confusion because of the women who were tied together. One wanted to go one way, and the next woman wanted to go another. Finally, things got sorted out so that they weren't continually pulling at one another's throats.

The children began gathering wood for fires while the men stumbled around in their neck yokes putting water and cornmeal in the cooking pots and setting them over the small fires to make the familiar porridge *nsima*.

With the situation under control, the Red Caps stayed back and allowed the captives to prepare their food without yelling and using their whips, except when one of the men got too near the edge of the clearing where he might try to run away into the jungle.

Wikatani and Chuma tried several times to talk to the new captives. The Ajawa language was similar enough to the Manganja language so that the boys could understand them speaking to one another. But the only response they received was angry glares; one woman close by spat on Wikatani.

"I know our tribes our enemies," Wikatani pouted, wiping off the spittle, "but *we* can't hurt them. Why are they so nasty to us?"

"I don't know," Chuma said, watching a Manganja girl in the glow of the light from the many small fires. She was about their age. "We are all captives of the Red Caps; we should help each other."

"Yes. We both have the same enemy now. The Red Caps don't belong here; they are outsiders." Wikatani was watching the same girl. She was pretty and not tied up like the older women.

When the girl looked their way, Chuma motioned to her to come over to them. She looked around to see if any Red Caps were watching, but she did not come. A few minutes later she looked at them again. Wikatani smiled, and she smiled back. He, too, motioned, but she shook her head.

Then she casually walked away from her people and began gathering wood near the edge of the clearing. Slowly she made her way around to the tree where Chuma and Wikatani were tied. "What do you want?" she asked when she was within hearing range.

"Water," they both said. "And food," added Chuma.

She walked on, picking up sticks until she got back to her family's fire.

In a few minutes the girl returned with a small gourd of water. "Have they not fed you?" she asked.

"Just a bone," said Wikatani.

"If this tree didn't have termites in it and a few grubs, we would have starved."

The girl looked closely at the boys. "You're not Manganja," she said in surprise.

"No. We're Ajawa," said Chuma. "The Red Caps captured us three days ago when we were taking our village sheep to pasture."

"The Ajawa are hyenas," the girl snapped. "They attack when one's back is turned." And she grabbed the water gourd and started to walk away.

"Wait!" said Wikatani. "Why do you say that?"

The girl turned slightly and gave them a hate-filled stare. She spoke in a tone of deep anger: "The Manganja and the Ajawa were supposed to be at peace. We kept the peace, but your people attacked us! In the dark I did not see that you are Ajawa, or I would never have brought you water."

Chuma thought fast. Their people had attacked the Manganja? He began to understand what had happened.

"But it was a mistake!" Chuma pleaded as the girl started to walk away again. "Our people thought *you* had captured us. That's why they went to war with you. They knew nothing about these Red Caps."

The girl hesitated.

Wikatani continued. "That's right. If our people had known that the Red Caps had captured us, they would have come here to rescue us."

The girl faced them again, still angry. "Why did the Ajawa think it was us?" she demanded.

"Who else?" said Wikatani.

"No; there's more to it than that," said Chuma. "The Red Caps broke a Manganja spear and left it on the trail where they caught us."

"And they spread blood all around to make it look as if we had been killed or badly hurt," added Wikatani.

"But why would the Red Caps do all that?" asked the girl skeptically.

"We think they *wanted* the Ajawa to attack the Manganja, so they made it look as if your tribe had captured us."

"But we don't know why," Wikatani admitted. "Why start a war between our two tribes?"

"If what you say is true," said the girl, "their reason is clear. They wanted to buy slaves. There are only five of them. So this was the only way to get many unarmed slaves."

"What do you mean?" asked Wikatani.

"We were captured by your people and taken to an Ajawa village. The Red Caps came the very next morning and bought all of us and brought us here."

"Bought you? With what?" asked Chuma.

"Rolls of bright colored cloth, pieces of copper wire, new cooking pots—white men's things," spat the girl.

Neither boy had ever seen a white man, but they had heard plenty of stories about them. Far down the Shire River, where it joined a larger river—the Zambezi—white men traveled on the water in their gigantic smoking canoes. Rumor said they had a village named *Tete* many miles up the Zambezi.

"Slave traders," breathed Wikatani. The only source of the brightly colored cloth, wire, and iron pots was white men. Often they traded those things for slaves.

A new fear shone in Wikatani's eyes. "Will we be sent away to the white man's land?"

"*We* won't," said the girl proudly. "Manganja warriors will soon rescue us."

"Yes. I'm sure they will try," said Chuma slowly, pondering the situation. "But they don't know where you are. They will attack Ajawa villages and take more captives in revenge—"

"And probably sell them to the Red Caps, too," added Wikatani.

The girl stared at the two boys in dismay. "Then . . . we might never get home!"

William Loren
Katz

The Fiery Abolitionists

With the help of abolitionists, an increasing number of enslaved African Americans were able to gain their freedom in the mid-1800s. African American historian William Loren Katz gives an overview of the climate of slavery in the United States in the time leading up to the Civil War.

IN THE 1850S, slaves increasingly heard news about the rising conflicts between North and South. By 1856, slaveholders reported their slaves were excited by the birth of a Republican Party dedicated to banning slavery in the West, and its presidential candidate, John Frémont. That year slaves also learned that whites in Kansas fought in armed battles over the future of bondage. A journalist in Kansas wrote: "The slaves are in a state of insurrection[1] all over the country."

Slaves in the South escaped in larger numbers than ever before, and more whites, particularly the poor, aided them and took part in slave conspiracies.[2] Panicky talk of black insurrections was heard in several states.

The Washington correspondent for the *New York Weekly Tribune* wrote in 1856 that "the insurrectionary movement in Tennessee" made "more headway than is known to the public" and insisted "important facts [were] being suppressed[3] in order to check the spread of the contagion."[4] The next week he told of serious outbreaks in New Orleans,

---

1. **insurrection** rebellion
2. **conspiracies** secret plans
3. **suppressed** held back
4. **contagion** corrupting influence

though local papers "carefully refrain[5] from any mention of the facts."

The *New Orleans Picayune* admitted it "refrained from publishing a great deal" about the "spirit of turbulence."[6] Two weeks later the *Picayune* said Christmas fires pointed to "slave plots" in Kentucky, Arkansas, Tennessee, Mississippi, Louisiana, and Texas. Its evidence added up to a "positive insurrection." . . .

Fugitives from border states slipped across the Mason-Dixon[7] line in large numbers. When the Ohio River froze, so many Kentucky runaways crossed the ice that congestion[8] became a problem. So many fugitives crowded into underground railroad stations in Lawrence, Kansas, in 1859, that its director, Colonel J. Bowles, desperately called for large amounts of financial aid.

The 1850s witnessed massive efforts to help escapees, including Harriet Tubman's nineteen trips. Jane Lewis went to Kentucky to help fugitives cross the river to freedom. Escapees Elizah Anderson and John Mason rescued more than two thousand. Mason was captured and sold back into slavery, but he escaped and continued his work. Former slave Arnold Cragston spent four years rowing hundreds from Kentucky across the Ohio River, saying, "We just knew there was a lot of slaves always a-wantin' to get free, and I had to help 'em." . . .

The abolitionist movement, inspired by slave resistance and determined to end the system one way or another, became increasingly revolutionary. By the 1850s, thousands of its black and white men and women members were helping runaways escape, challenging federal efforts to return fugitives, and discussing slavery's violent overthrow in the South.

On abolition's cutting edge was John Brown, a man of action. A devout Christian who identified fully with African Americans, he planned to seize the federal arsenal[9] at Harpers Ferry, Virginia (later West Virginia), and help launch black maroon[10] colonies in the Alleghenies. Brown told Frederick Douglass these mountains were placed by God "to aid the emancipation of your race." Douglass admired Brown's courage

---

5. **refrain** stay away

6. **turbulence** disorder; unrest

7. **Mason-Dixon line** boundary between Pennsylvania and Maryland, regarded as the division between the free and slave states

8. **congestion** overcrowding

9. **arsenal** storage center for weapons

10. **maroon** person who has escaped enslavement

but warned him he was heading into a "perfect steel trap."

On October 16, 1859, Brown led a band of twenty-two that included five blacks and seventeen whites, including his own sons. Two black recruits had been charged in the Oberlin rescue: John Copeland, an Oberlin student, and Copeland's uncle, Lewis Sheridan Leary (an ancestor of poet Langston Hughes).

U.S. troops commanded by Col. Robert E. Lee and Lt. J. E. B. Stuart trapped Brown and his men. Ten were killed, seven (including Brown) were captured, and five escaped. However, the assault proved some whites were willing to die fighting slavery.

The quiet courage and thoughtful words of Brown during the forty days before his execution stirred the world and placed emancipation on the national agenda.[11] In France, Victor Hugo called him "an apostle[12] and a hero" and a "martyr."[13] Poet James Russell Lowell said: "But that scaffold[14] sways the future."

In 1860, President Lincoln and the Republican Party won the presidency. Those who owned slaves no longer dictated U.S. policy. Eleven southern states threatened to secede from the Union and form their own confederacy. Bishop Elliot of Savannah announced that self-government and equality were "great falsehoods." Confederate vice president Alexander H. Stephens's inauguration speech called slavery "the great truth" and stated that "freedom is not possible without slavery."

Once slaveholders claimed they were pious,[15] democratic gentlemen. They still felt that way about themselves. But in 1861, many northerners realized slaveholders were far more committed to slavery than democracy. To protect slavery they would ignore rights for which Americans had fought and died.

---

11. **agenda** list of things to be done; program
12. **apostle** pioneer of moral reform
13. **martyr** one who suffers for a belief
14. **scaffold** platform used in the execution of a condemned prisoner
15. **pious** religious

Frances E. W. Harper

Bury Me in a Free Land

These poems written by Frances E. W. Harper and Langston Hughes reflect the tragic legacy of slavery.

Make me a grave where'er you will,
In a lowly plain, or a lofty hill;
Make it among earth's humblest graves,
But not in a land where men are slaves.

5   I could not rest if around my grave
I heard the steps of a trembling slave;
His shadow above my silent tomb
Would make it a place of fearful gloom.

I could not rest if I heard the tread
10   Of a coffle[1] gang to the shambles[2] led,
And the mother's shriek of wild despair
Rise like a curse on the trembling air.

I could not sleep if I saw the lash
Drinking her blood at each fearful gash,
15   And I saw her babes torn from her breast,
Like trembling doves from their parent nest.

---

1. **coffle** train of slaves
2. **shambles** slave market

I'd shudder and start if I heard the bay
Of bloodhounds seizing their human prey,
And I heard the captive plead in vain
20   As they bound afresh his galling[3] chain.

If I saw young girls from their mothers' arms
Bartered and sold for their youthful charms,
My eye would flash with a mournful flame,
My death-paled cheek grow red with shame.

25   I would sleep, dear friends, where bloated[4] might[5]
Can rob no man of his dearest right;
My rest shall be calm in any grave
Where none can call his brother a slave.

I ask no monument, proud and high,
30   To arrest the gaze of the passers-by;
All that my yearning spirit craves,
Is bury me not in a land of slaves.

---

3. **galling** irritating
4. **bloated** puffed up
5. **might** force

Langston Hughes

Afro-American Fragment

So long,
So far away
Is Africa.
Not even memories alive
5   Save those that history books create,
Save those that songs
Beat back into the blood—
Beat out of blood with words sad-sung
In strange un-Negro tongue—
10   So long,
So far away
Is Africa.

Subdued[1] and time-lost
Are the drums—and yet
15   Through some vast mist of race
There comes this song
I do not understand,
This song of atavistic[2] land,
Of bitter yearnings lost
20   Without a place—
So long,
So far away
Is Africa's
Dark face.

___

1. **subdued** hushed
2. **atavistic** reappearing with ancestral qualities

**Langston
Hughes**

American Heartbreak

I am the American heartbreak—
Rock on which Freedom
Stumps its toe—
The great mistake
5   That Jamestown
Made long ago.

**Interviewed by
Leta Gray**

Clayton Holbert
Ottawa, Kansas

In this reading, Leta Gray interviews Clayton Holbert, a former enslaved African American, who tells her of daily life during slavery and the years after, known as Reconstruction. Holbert's account explains a little about what the enslaved people on a boat such as The Moonlight *could expect from life in the United States.*

MY NAME IS CLAYTON HOLBERT, and I am an ex-slave. I am eighty-six years old. I was born and raised in Linn County, Tennessee. My master's name was Pleasant "Ples" Holbert. My master had a fairly large plantation; he had, I imagine, around one hundred slaves.

I was working the fields during the wind-up of the Civil War. They always had a man in the field to teach the small boys to work, and I was one of the boys. I was learning to plant corn, etc. My father, brother and uncle went to war on the Union side.

We raised corn, barley, and cotton, and produced all of our living on the plantation. There was no such thing as going to town to buy things. All of our clothing was homespun, our socks were knitted, and everything. We had our looms, and made our own suits, we also had reels, and we carved, spun, and knitted. We always wore yarn socks for winter, which we made. It didn't get cold, in the winter in Tennessee, just a little frost was all. We fixed all of our cotton and wool ourselves.

For our meat we used to kill fifteen, twenty, or fifty, and sometimes a hundred hogs. We usually had hickory. It was considered the best for smoking meat, when we butchered. Our meat we had then was the finest possible. It had a lot more flavor than that which you get now.

If a person ran out of meat, he would go over to his neighbor's house, and borrow or buy meat, we didn't think about going to town. . . .

We made our own maple syrup from the maple sugar trees. This is a lot better than the refined sugar people have nowadays, and is good for you too. You can't get this now though, except sometimes and it is awfully high priced. On the plantations the slaves usually had a house of their own for their families. They usually built their houses in a cir-cle, so you didn't have to go out doors hardly to go to the house next to you. If you wanted your house away from the rest of the houses, they could build you a house away from the others and separate.

I was never sold, I always had just my one master. When slave owners died, if they had no near relatives to inherit their property, they would 'Will' the slaves their freedom, instead of giving them to someone else. . . .

The slaves used to dance or go to the prayer meeting to pass their time. There were also festivals we went to, during the Christmas vaca-tion. There was always a big celebration on Christmas. We worked until Christmas Eve and from that time until New Year's we had a vacation. We had no such thing as Thanksgiving, we had never heard of such a thing.

In August when it was the hottest we always had a vacation after our crops were all laid by. That was the time when we usually had several picnics, barbecues or anything we wanted to do to pass our time away.

After the war was over, and my father, brother and uncle had gone to war, [the war] left my mother alone practically. My mother had always been a cook, and that was all she knew, and after the war she got her freedom, she and me, I was seven or eight years old, and my brother was fourteen, and my sister was about sixteen. My mother didn't know what to do, and I guess we looked kind of pitiful, finally my master said that we could stay and work for him a year, and then we also stayed there the following year, and he paid us the second year. After that we went to another place, Roof Macaroy, and then my sister got married while we were there, and then she moved on her husband's master's place, and then we went too. After that I moved on another part and farmed for two or three years, and then we moved to another part of the plantation and lived there three or four years. That was almost the cen-ter of things, and we held church there. All of the colored people would gather there. The colored people who had been in the North were bet-ter educated than the people in the South. They would come down to the South and help the rest of us. The white people would also try to promote religion among the colored people. Our church was a big log cabin. We lived in it, but we moved from one of the large rooms into a small one, so we could have church. I remember one time after we had been down on the creek bank fishing, that was what we always did on Sunday, because we didn't know any better; my master called us boys and told us we should go to Sunday school instead of going fishing. I remember that to this day, and I have only been fishing one or two times since. Then I didn't know what he was talking about. But two or three years later I learned what Sunday school was and I started to go.

I went to a subscription school. We would all pay a man to come to teach us. I used to work for my room and board on Saturdays, and go to school five days a week. That would have been all right, if I had kept it up, but I didn't for very long, I learned to read and write pretty good though. There were no Government schools then that were free.

We didn't have a name. The slaves were always known by the master's last name, and after we were freed we just took the last name of our masters and used it. After we had got our freedom papers, they had our ages and all on them, they were lost so we guess at our ages. . . .

In 1877 a lot of people began coming out here to Kansas and in 1878 there were several, but in 1879 there were an awful lot of colored people immigrating. We came in 1877 to Kansas City, October 1. We landed about midnight. We came by train. Then there was nothing but little huts in the bottoms. The Santa Fe depot didn't amount to anything. The Armours' Packing house was ever smaller than that. There was a swinging bridge over the river. The Raw Valley was considered good-for-nothing, but to raise hemp. There was an awful lot of it grown there though, and there were also beavers in the Kaw River, and they used to cut down trees to build their dams. I worked several years and in 1890 I came to Franklin County. . . .

I was about twenty-two years old when I married, and I have raised six children. They live over by Appanoose, I ruined my health hauling wood. I was always a big fellow, I used to weigh over two hundred eighty-five pounds, but I worked too hard, working both summer and winter.

My father's mother lived 'til she was around ninety or a hundred years old. She got so bent at the last she was practically bent double. She lived about two years after she was set free.

I used to live up around Appanoose, but I came to Franklin County and I have stayed here ever since.

Captain
Scott O'Grady

from
Return with Honor

United States Air Force Captain Scott O'Grady was shot down while flying over Bosnia in 1995. Captain O'Grady recalls the techniques he used to survive both the elements and the enemies as he waited to be rescued.

It WAS STILL DARK AS INK Tuesday morning when I woke from a doze to an explosion that shook the ground and gave me the shock of my life. It sounded like incoming fire, no more than fifty yards west.

I hunkered down inside my tarp.[1] My mind ran wild. Did they know where I was—or were they trying to ferret[2] me out? Was it a mortar?[3] A hand grenade?

It took me a while to get a grip—to realize that what I'd heard was not the landing of a shell, but perhaps an artillery recoil[4]—or, from what I'd be told later, the sonic boom[5] of a very low flying jet.

The night returned to normal. But that bizarre wake-up call, along with the visit of the cows the day before, convinced me to keep moving south and over the big hill. My hole-up site was a disaster waiting to happen. And even if I chanced to make radio contact here and transmit my coordinates,[6] it was no place to stage a rescue mission.

---

1. **tarp** canvas covering
2. **ferret** search out
3. **mortar** small cannon
4. **artillery recoil** kickback from a fired gun
5. **sonic boom** sound resembling an explosion
6. **coordinates** set of numbers indicating exact location on a map

But I wasn't going anywhere yet, not until the next night. I could tell by the birdcall that dawn was closing in. The sun would be up by five o'clock. Not that I was timing it; I'd scarcely looked at my watch of late, kept its shiny metal hidden under the sleeve of my flight suit.

The passage of time no longer held the same meaning for me. I marked the daily cycles—the low clouds rolling in at midmorning, the afternoon rains, the spotty gunfire in the distance just before sundown. But beyond those, time was a trivial item. My nights became days and my days became nights, since my main activities—movement and radio talk—were reserved for after dark. I had no sleep cycle to speak of; I was getting an hour or two per day in snatches. I had no office to show up at, no errands to run, no dinner dates to prepare for, no TV shows to look forward to. I had nothing better to do than to live. To survive. That was a full-time job and then some, and I did it one minute at a time.

On the other hand, I wasn't ignoring the passing of the days. I knew it was Tuesday, June 6, and that I was into my fifth day of evasion.[7] I wasn't particularly hungry; a stomach shrinks fast when you put nothing in it. But I had to keep my strength up for that forty-five-day siege,[8] if need be. I ate a few more leaves—the oval kind, not the hairy ones on the thistle bushes—and they weren't any tastier or moister than before. Then I saw an ant crawl by my head, and one of those cartoon lightbulbs went on inside.

I knew that most insects are edible. In much of the world, in fact, they are viewed as healthy taste treats: high in fat and salt, more protein than beef, chock full of vitamins and minerals. In Africa and Asia, where meat is unaffordable for many, the big beetles are especially popular—they're supposed to have a nutty flavor when roasted.

I went through Air Force survival training in winter, when the bugs were gone, and I'd never eaten so much as a termite. But now opportunity knocked, and I was on the prowl. The spiders and bees I'd come across didn't perk my appetite. Had I run into a cricket, I'd have peeled off its head and legs and wings, all the hard parts, and mucked it down. But the Bosnian crickets, though they raised a racket, stayed out of eyeshot.

Which left me with the ants.

---

7. **evasion** escape
8. **siege** continued attack

They were good-sized bugs, with reddish heads and brown bodies, and I'd seen two or three of them crawl around me the day before. This time I followed the straggler's path. It developed that he was joining a feast two feet past my head, where about twenty of his friends were chowing down on a decaying worm. I watched for a while, lying on my left side, mulling[9] my move—were they fire ants? would they sting me?—before reaching out with my mittened right hand. As soon as one of the ants crawled on the mitten, I squished it between my fist and my rucksack.[10]

Making sure it was dead, I took off my mitten, picked it up with my fingers, and—here went nothing—popped it whole into my mouth. There are honey ants so sweet that children cry for them for dessert, but this guy was sour as lemon. I waited two minutes for a reaction, then crunched him up and swallowed.

After that we were off to the races. My first kill had set off the alarm, and the remaining ants were running every which way. That made them more difficult to trap, but I got the hang of it. I became a squishing machine. Within a half hour I'd thrown down fifteen of them.

I didn't experience the least bit of food aversion;[11] I'd have eaten a plateful if it had been served to me. There isn't much bulk to an ant, and the episode was worth more in entertainment than nutrition. It was one of my rare mental breaks.

And I can't deny that it was nice to be the hunter for a change.

I heard a jet again that afternoon and monitored my radio when I could, but nothing came through. Later on I made out the report of a far helicopter and the cracking boom that had shocked me, now well off to the east.

With a few hours left till sunset, I prepped for my night move. For maximum concealment, I applied some green and brown camo[12] paste to my face. The ski mask was still valuable—you lose 70 percent of your body heat through an uncovered head—but its hole had sagged, till it drooped below my mouth. The camo—and my growing beard—would prevent my skin tone from betraying me.

---

9. **mulling** thinking over
10. **rucksack** knapsack
11. **aversion** dislike
12. **camo** camouflage

Then I heard a familiar, heavy clomping down the path and a clanging bell behind it. It was Leroy and Alfred, and this time they'd brought along their pal, Tinker Bell. *A fine job of hiding you've done,* I told myself. *You picked the cows' favorite dining spot.*

I buried my face into the tarp, too fearful to peek out, hoping against hope that the cows would pass me by this time. But I'd have no such luck—it was like a nightmare I couldn't shake. Leroy and Alfred were creatures of habit. They cut across the cove the same way, barreled straight toward my thistle patch, stopped two yards from my feet. Their noise was the same; it felt like it came at me from 360 degrees. Their table manners were just as gross—the word "grazing" didn't do justice to that sloppy hubbub they made.

I couldn't believe it. I'd somehow survived a supersonic missile, a last-ditch ejection, a parachute ride from higher than the top of Mount McKinley, and several platoons[13] of rifle-toting[14] paramilitaries.[15] And now I might be defeated by a pair of stupid cows.

If that wasn't enough to tick me off, there was Tinker Bell, ding-donging like a maniac on the opposite side of the cove. At a hundred feet, that bell was a killer. The only thing worse than hearing it ring was hearing it occasionally stop; I'd imagine that Tinker Bell had spotted me and taken off to get his buddies. But the bell never stopped clanging for long.

I thought about what I might do if the herder confronted me. Run for the hills? That sounded right. Overpower him if he got in my way? I could try, though I didn't feel up to two falls out of three. Use the Beretta?[16] Bad idea—the shot would bring people in from all around, and they wouldn't be feeling kindly toward me.

Please, God, don't let him find me. Keep me safe until sundown, till I can find my way out.

After a half hour's snack, Leroy and Alfred crashed off—out of the cove, down the path, with Tinker Bell hot behind them. Why they left was a mystery, but I knew that the next time I saw a cow it had better be on a plate, medium rare.

---

13. **platoons** parts of a military company
14. **rifle-toting** rifle-carrying
15. **paramilitaries** civilians organized in a military fashion
16. **Beretta** type of gun

Hours after dark, when the land had settled, I packed up my gear and left the thistle patch. I got tripped up more than once moving out of that thicket, nearly fell on my face. I stepped on more dead branches in thirty minutes than I had in four days. But I made it out.

I was on the watch for a dirt path that might have channeled[17] an artillery piece and the soldiers to man it—that was a path I didn't want to cross. I moved along small, flat fields, bordered by bushy trees—sometimes east, sometimes south, wherever the terrain took me. A ripe moon half lit my way, and the Big Dipper was out again, but my zigzagging got me disoriented, even with my compass out. I tried to get references off the big hill, now visible to the south, but there was more than one hill out there, and it was hard to correlate[18] what I saw with what I recalled from my evasion chart.

I felt like I'd been let out of a closet and into a strange, dark house.

How many nights would I be stumbling along like this? How far would I have to go to be rescued? I didn't let the questions hang: as long as it took. I had to be willing to walk back to Croatia if need be—through mountain passes and cities and enemy forces. It might take me a year or two, but I could do it.

Anxious to see if Flashman or someone else was up there, I monitored on Guard as I moved. But when I used the earpiece, my inner ear would magnify the sound of my own breathing, masking the sounds around me—a dangerous proposition. I took out the earpiece, turned the radio off.

Creeping through the shadows, I moved onto a game path forged[19] by people or cows. I came upon a series of stone walls, no more than three feet high, and clambered over them. The vegetation thickened. I neared a large stand of trees, where my path became two, circling round in either direction. I was pondering which branch to take when I heard a small splash and felt my ripped right boot fill with water; I'd stepped in a muddy puddle. Muttering a silent oath, I slogged on to the left, and it was then I made my first glaring error in judgment since deserting my hit-and-run kit at my landing site.

By that point I'd depleted[20] my water again. There'd been no rain

---

17. **channeled** conveyed
18. **correlate** connect
19. **forged** formed
20. **depleted** used up

to speak of since the thunderstorm. I'd tried sponging up dew, but it was hardly worth the effort. I'd kept a mouthful or two of water in the travel pouch in reserve, for morale's sake, but I hadn't drunk any all day long.

It would have been easy enough to submerge the pouch in the puddle, then purify the muddy water later on with iodine tablets from my survival vest. It just slipped my mind. I was mad about my wet boot and preoccupied about where I was headed.

I had a new strategy for my next hole-up site. Rather than keep moving till dawn, I'd stop an hour or more before sunrise, leaving me time to scout out the best spot and feel more secure. The time came as I reached another short stone fence, running north to south. To its east I could see the lighter grays of open pastures. On the west side, where I was, there were lots of young trees and thick bushes. It seemed logical that any cows would graze on the open side; they weren't likely to hurdle a wall.

I settled on a sheltered spot a hundred feet from the fence—the kind of place, I thought, where a guy might bring his lady for a picnic in the woods. I broke off some more branches for extra concealment and placed a leafy one over my feet.

It felt like I'd trekked over three time zones since that first pell-mell dash, fresh from the parachute. In fact, I'd traveled less than two miles from my landing site.

By the time I bedded down, it was too light to try transmitting; that would wait one more day. According to SAR[21] procedures, after all, it was up to NATO[22] to initiate the radio call; the more often I called in the clear, the greater my risk of detection. As before, I would limit myself to monitoring until well after dark.

As eager as I was for rescue, I stayed patient. I felt I'd have just one shot, and I was going to do it right. No matter how slowly the hours dragged by, a week of evasion—or a month, or more—wasn't much of a sacrifice. Not when you weighed it against the chance of captivity, when the clocks could stop for years, or for good.

While this third hole-up site was my best yet, the new digs were less than deluxe. I spent the first part of that morning excavating softball-sized rocks that dug into my side, and the rest of it managing my camouflage. There were lots of dead low branches on the near

---

21. **SAR** search and rescue

22. **NATO** North American Treaty Organization, an alliance established among various European and North American countries with the goal of protecting each other and promoting stability in Europe

trees, and they'd disintegrate at the lightest touch.

Other than that, I was happy with my new address. I could hear cows and people beyond the stone fence, but no closer. I had wearied of company, and it looked like I'd left it behind.

I'd never been much of a camper, even as a kid. The mosquitoes liked me too much, for one thing. (A great blessing in Bosnia was the absence of biting insects.) Whenever I spent a night in the wild, I was always glad to retreat to a cabin with a real bathroom. Now, after five days in the great outdoors, I felt filthy. I'd have done bodily harm for a shower. I'd have paid a year's salary to brush my teeth—they felt like they had socks on.

The worst was the cold. I'd been shivering on and off for a while, and now my body was shaking. I kept wishing for sun, if only to lay out my socks to dry, but the skies weren't cooperating. My boots were full of water—they felt as wet as my mouth felt dry. I'd planned to wait till dark to remove them, but by early evening I couldn't stand it anymore; I had to air those boots out. I pulled them off, then peeled away my soaked, yellowing socks. I inspected my feet for frostbite; I'd had frostbite once at the age of twelve, when my chairlift stalled on a ski slope, and now I checked for the telltale white patches. None were visible—a big relief. But my toes were shriveled like raisins, and almost numb. I tried to warm them with my wool mittens.

Then I did something I never would have believed one week before. I took those wet woolen socks and wrung them out into a ziplock bag. The water was rusty brown, about the color of mushroom soup, and there was less than an ounce of it. The flavor was even worse than you'd expect, but I was *thirsty*, and my small drink encouraged me.

I would keep making my way, by any means available.

I lapsed into a combat nap . . . and into one of those dreams born from wanting something so bad that your subconscious constructs it. I dreamt that it was okay to come out of hiding—that a safe recovery point had been prearranged with the United Nations. That the local farmers were sympathetic Muslims. That I could give myself up to the next person I saw and he'd get me dinner and a bed. That someone would pick me up the next day and drive me out of the war—

It was just a five-minute mental vacation, a break from the grind of evasion, but I pulled myself awake to cut it off.

I checked my tarp, my netting, the branches that cloaked me, and resumed my wait for the dark.